MW00916598

STYLE

New York Times Bestselling Author

CHELSEA M. CAMERON

Style
Copyright © 2016 Chelsea M. Cameron
All Rights Reserved.
ISBN-10: 1533504903
ISBN-13: 978-1533504906
Editing by Laura Helseth
Cover by KassiJean
Formatting by Midnight Engel Press, LLC
chelseamcameron.com

Style is a work of fiction. Names, characters, places and incidents are either the product of the author's imagination or are use fictitiously. Any resemblance to actual persons, living or dead, events, business establishments or locales is entirely coincidental.

No part of this book may be reproduced, scanned or distributed in any printed or electronic form without permission. All rights reserved.

NOVELS BY THE AUTHOR

Nocturnal (The Noctalis Chronicles, Book One)

Amazon

Nightmare (The Noctalis Chronicles, Book Two)

Amazon

Neither (The Noctalis Chronicles, Book Three)

Amazon

Neverend (The Noctalis Chronicles, Book Four)

Amazon

Whisper (The Whisper Trilogy, Book One)

Amazon Barnes and Noble Kobo

Deeper We Fall (Fall and Rise, Book One)

Amazon Barnes and Noble Kobo iBooks

Faster We Burn (Fall and Rise, Book Two)

Amazon Barnes and Noble Kobo iBooks

Together We Heal

Amazon Barnes and Noble Kobo iBooks

My Favorite Mistake (Available from Harlequin)

Amazon Barnes and Noble Kobo iBooks

My Sweetest Escape (Available from Harlequin)

Amazon Barnes and Noble Kobo iBooks

Our Favorite Days (My Favorite Mistake, Book Three)

Amazon Barnes and Noble Kobo iBooks

Sweet Surrendering

Amazon Barnes and Noble Kobo iBooks

Surrendering to Us

Amazon Barnes and Noble Kobo iBooks

Dark Surrendering

Amazon Barnes and Noble KoboiBooks

For Real (Rules of Love, Book One)

Amazon Barnes and Noble Kobo iBooks

For Now (Rules of Love, Book Two)

Amazon Barnes and Noble Kobo iBooks

Deep Surrendering

Amazon

<u>**UnWritten**</u>

Amazon Barnes and Noble Kobo iBooks

Behind Your Back

Amazon Barnes and Noble Kobo iBooks

Back to Back

Amazon Barnes and Noble Kobo iBooks

Bend Me, Break Me

Amazon

Contact The Author

www.chelseamcameron.com

Twitter: @chel_c_cam

Facebook: Chelsea M. Cameron (Official Author Page)

TEXT
ILOVE TO 66866

TO BE ADDED TO
THE MAILING LIST FOR CHELSEA M. CAMERON

DEDICATION

For all the girls who like girls.
This one's for you.

CHAPTER 1

"She's like . . . Satan in a blonde package," Grace said as Stella Lewis walked by. Grace had it right. I slammed my locker and leaned my back against it as Stella went around the corner, her skirt flipping, but not showing *too* much. Just enough. Her ash-blonde hair was curled perfectly, as if she had a team of stylists in her home to get her ready every day.

"Well, I don't think she's *that* evil. Just . . . driven? Assertive?" Grace just rolled her eyes.

"Those are just other words for 'bitch', Kyle." I shrugged as we walked beside each other to class. A few people stared as we went by, but I ignored them. Grace had the misfortune of being one of the only black girls at a small high school in Maine; and then there was me. They looked because I walked with a visible limp, mostly due to the fact that one of my legs was longer than the other, and even with multiple surgeries to lengthen it, there was still a discrepancy. Not to mention the scars. It was so much better than it had been, but in high school any physical anomaly was reason to stare, especially in a homogenous community.

I took my messy bun down and then put it back up again. It was a habit I had when I was annoyed by something. Or nervous. Or stressed.

Or tired. Grace took the seat next to me in AP Chemistry and sighed.

"What?" I asked, hauling out the enormous textbook and dropping it with a thud on my desk.

"Nothing. Just thinking." She pushed her dark curls out of her face and glared up at them.

"Be careful. That could be dangerous," I said, pushing my black-rimmed glasses up my nose. Yeah, yeah, I was the stereotype. Girl who loved academics and wore glasses. I'd heard all the jokes before, so save it.

Something was bothering her, and as usual, she was going to hold it in until she couldn't stand it anymore and then it would burst out of her at a totally inopportune time. Like when we were in the middle of dinner with my parents. Or at the movies. Or in the library. Or in the middle of a test.

"Whatever," she said, pulling out her Chapstick and slicking it on her lips. Mrs. Collins started class and I knew I was going to have to wait.

We were working on diagramming chemical bonds, so I let my brain be taken over by that and pushed Grace's potential problem to the side. Science wasn't my best subject, but I did well enough to make it to AP Chemistry my senior year, so that had to count for something. Grace and I split up, her to head to Art and me to AP Geometry and then we met up again outside the cafeteria. Like always.

We got in line and filled our trays with pizza, and I decided to grab a salad because pizza and salad cancelled each other out. By the time we got back to the table, Molly, her boyfriend Tommy, Paige, Monica, and Chris were already eating.

"Whoa, what's with Grace?" Molly whispered in my ear as Grace glowered at her food like it had offended her in some way.

"No idea," I said back as Tommy and Chris debated something politics-related that would probably end in them agreeing to disagree. Again.

"Hey, is anyone going to the game on Friday?" Monica asked.

She, Chris, and Molly were in the band playing flute, bass drum, and clarinet respectively.

"Yeah, sure," I said. I tried to make most of the games to support them, and we all showed up for Grace and Monica when the drama club put on productions. My friends were pretty spectacular and I didn't know what I would have done without them.

"Everyone else in?" Monica asked, and we all agreed. I couldn't have cared less about the actual sport (football), so I usually brought a book and only looked up or paid attention when the band was doing something.

Don't get me wrong, sports are fine, but they're not really my forte, considering running isn't my thing and most of them require it. I would much rather spend my time reading or . . . doing anything else.

"What the hell?" Grace said, finally looking up and turning toward a commotion on the other side of the cafeteria.

"Oh God, what are they doing now?" I said. It was one of the tables for the football players and they were always up to something. Brad Harding was standing on top of one of the tables and chugging . . . something from a glass bottle.

"What is that?" I said, squinting.

"I think it's hot sauce," Molly said, shaking her head.

Yup, definitely hot sauce. Brad's face got red, he started gagging and then hurled all over the table before one of the lunch monitors hauled him off the table and down the hall to the principal's office. A surly custodian came over to clean up as groups of students clapped in support.

I was about to turn and say something to Grace when my gaze snagged on Stella. She stood with her arms crossed as she rolled her eyes. Tossing her hair over one shoulder, she just happened to look in my direction and catch me staring. I looked away fast, so she didn't think I was . . . well, anyway.

"I can't believe people think that's funny. I mean, how old are they?" Grace said, her brows furrowed. If she didn't tell me what was up by the end of the day, I was going to confront her. Because this was downright ridiculous.

"Well, he's going to get suspended, again," I said. Brad got suspended a lot, but it never stuck because his dad was a lawyer *and* a former politician *and* crazy rich. So Brad was basically the worst because he could get away with it.

The topic changed from Brad's idiocy to Homecoming weekend and I checked out. It wasn't that I didn't care ...

Okay, that *was* it. I just couldn't get so whooped up about something that didn't really mean anything. These weren't the best days of our lives. I was always looking forward to college. If I could just get to college, I knew my life would start.

I'd finally get a boyfriend and my obsession with academia would be appreciated and I'd be out on my own. Not that I didn't adore my parents, but I was an only child and living with their expectations hanging over my head had been intense, to say the least. Good thing I was smart, or else I would have had to work my ass off at something else to meet their expectations of being an extraordinary child.

College was going to be it. I just had to get to graduation and then I would be free.

⸻◆⸻

Instead of heading home after school, I always took my laptop downtown to the library and got most of my homework done. It was a hell of a lot easier to work on everything when I didn't have one (or both) of my parents leaning over my shoulder asking what I was doing and if I was sure I wanted to use that exact word, or if that number was right. They put the *hel* in helicopter parenting.

After I finished everything I needed to get done homework wise, I let myself do some work. Last summer I'd gotten a job at a small IT support company in town and my boss, Jason, had taught me a little bit of coding and graphic design, so I'd started doing a few freelance jobs here and there. Just basic stuff like Photoshop editing and basic web design, but you could make pretty decent money at it. I wasn't sure if it was what I wanted to do when I got to college, but if I could make a few bucks and enjoy what I was doing, then why not?

My current project was a blog redesign for a new book blogger. I hadn't even known book blogging was a thing until I posted some of my ads in online forums. She was also a senior in high school and didn't have a whole lot of money, so she couldn't hire a real professional. We'd exchanged emails back and forth and I'd liked her and knew I could give her a great design. She'd already done part of the work; finding me stock images and colors and fonts that she wanted to use.

I'd just gotten started, but she was happy with the progress. I put on my coding playlist (which included everything from Adele to the Hamilton soundtrack to Muse) and before I knew it, the head librarian was tapping me on the shoulder and kicking me out.

Time to go home.

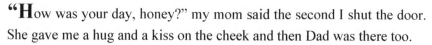

"**H**ow was your day, honey?" my mom said the second I shut the door. She gave me a hug and a kiss on the cheek and then Dad was there too.

"Fine," I said, knowing that wasn't an acceptable answer. She gave me the Mom Look and I sighed internally.

"It was good. Got a 98 on my AP Chem quiz and Mr. Hurley assigned us *Jane Eyre* for our next book." I would be asked to give many more specifics, but that would happen at the dinner table.

To be fair to my parents, they did only want the best for me. Neither of them had gone to college, but had been almost entirely self-taught and didn't want me to struggle like they had. Granted, the economy was a hell of a lot different now than it was when they were growing up, but I didn't want to burst that bubble. In the end, we both wanted the same thing. Me, at a good college and getting at least a master's degree. In . . . something.

Still figuring that out.

"I'm going to take a shower," I announced and escaped to my bathroom for a reprieve.

My room was kind of a disaster, as usual. I nearly tripped over a pair of sweatpants on my way to the bathroom. Might be time to do some laundry. I picked them up and tossed them on top of the overflowing hamper.

I turned the water on nearly all the way and stepped under, yelping a little. No doubt when I got out there would be no hot water. I was a fan of long showers, especially when my parents wanted to ask me to describe every moment of my day.

I closed my eyes and leaned my head back, letting the water soak my hair. Sighing, I slid my hand down my stomach and between my legs. I was paranoid that my parents would hear me somehow, so the shower was ideal for "relieving stress." It probably wasted water, but whatever.

I kept my eyes closed and ran my fingers up and down the inside of my thighs. As always, I tried to picture my ideal man. I needed some sort of visual stimulation to get off. I created him in painstaking detail, but it just wasn't working. He was . . . blurry. I stroked myself and tried harder. He would have blonde hair and wasn't too muscular, just enough so that you knew he probably ran or did some sort of activity. He had a sexy voice and didn't call me "baby" because that was patronizing. He had just a few tattoos on his chest.

I growled in frustration. It wasn't working. There was just too much on my mind to get myself there. That had been happening more and more lately. Stupid stress. Stupid senior year messing with my masturbation. I opened my eyes and gave up. Maybe I'd try again later when I was in bed.

My mind drifted to other things as I washed my hair. I replayed the day and for some reason, I kept seeing Stella walking by me this morning. Like my brain was stuck and just kept replaying it.

What the hell? I shook my head and shoved it aside, but the moment I did, there was a twisting in the pit of my stomach. My heart started to race, as if I was running from something, and I quickly finished my shower and got out.

After I scrubbed myself with the towel so hard that my skin was red and raw I yanked a brush through my hair. It snagged more than a few times and I ripped out a few hairs. I told myself to calm the fuck down and get my shit together. It was nothing.

It was totally nothing.

***

Stella

"Pull up, pull up, you've almost got it," I said to Joy as she attempted to hit her scorpion. She was so close to having her back arched perfectly with her foot pulled behind her head. Almost. Just a bit more stretching and she'd have it.

She made a face at me and then let her foot snap back to the floor.

"I feel like I'm bending myself in two," she said, getting down on the floor to work on her splits.

"Well, you kind of are," I said, getting down on the mat and joining her. As a senior captain of the cheer squad, one of my jobs was to take some of the JV girls under my wing and help them out. Sort of like a big sister/little sister situation. It could be kind of a pain in the ass, but at least Joy wasn't obnoxious and really seemed like she wanted to listen to what I had to say.

After we stretched, we hit the locker room. Our big/little time was supposed to happen outside of practice, so we had to work it around both our schedules. If I didn't hurry, I was going to be very late for work, so I took a quick "baby wipe shower," changed my clothes, and said goodbye to Joy before rushing to my car. I knew I was sweaty and my hair was a mess, but that couldn't be helped.

I pulled into the vet's office and I was two minutes late. Shit. I dashed in the back door and nearly crashed into Maggie, who was dealing with a very grumpy golden retriever who didn't want to be doing whatever she was trying to get it to do.

"Sorry!" I said as I nearly tripped over the leash and we got tangled together. I regained my balance and we untangled ourselves as the dog moaned and groaned.

"What are you doing to this poor boy?" I asked.

"Giving him shots. I'm a terrible person, aren't I, Gunnar?" We both looked down at the dog as he howled like we were murdering him. I just laughed and moved past her to the back room where I could stash my bag. My scrubs today had little hearts on them. I'd gotten them around Valentine's Day, but I figured hearts could be worn year round. I hustled to the front desk where the receptionist, Margie, gave me a look.

"Sorry, sorry," I said, sitting down and booting up my computer. It was one of those terrible ancient desktops that was roughly the equivalent of a computer dinosaur, but the clinic didn't have a lot of extra funds for new computers.

I signed in and got to work. Since I wasn't even a vet tech, I didn't get to interact much with the animals outside of checking them, and their owners, in. Most of my job involved boring clerical work, but if I wanted to get into vet school, this was one of the first steps.

I worked on schedules, checked people out, filed, organized, and did a bunch of other little tasks, and soon it was time to clock out. That was one of the reasons I loved it. Never a dull moment. I ended up breaking up a potential fight between a dog and a very old, very mean cat whose owner refused to use a cat carrier, and then ended up consoling a girl whose hamster was put to sleep.

"Busy day," Margie said as I organized my desk again. I wanted it to look the same every day when I came back. I was weird that way.

"Same as always," I said, giving her a little wave. "See you tomorrow." She covered a yawn with her hand and I made my way into the back to grab my stuff. A few of the dogs who were there for overnight observation barked as I went by, begging me to release them.

"Not today, guys," I said, but they didn't listen and kept barking. My stomach yelled at me as I got in my car and turned it on. Shit. I was almost out of gas.

"Perfect," I sighed. Just one more thing I had to do today.

"I'm home," I called an hour later when I came through the door with a few bags of groceries.

"Hey, Star," Dad said as I dropped the bags in the kitchen and gave him a quick hug, then he started helping me put everything away.

"How was work?" he asked, putting the cereal box on the wrong shelf. He didn't appreciate my organizational skills, but that was fine. I'd arrange them correctly later.

I filled him in on my day and asked how his had been.

"Good, good. I assigned *Hamlet* today so we'll see how that goes." He rolled his eyes and I laughed. He was an English professor at the local community college and needless to say, a lot of the students in his classes weren't exactly fans of literature. They were forced to take English and liked to punish my dad when he tried to teach them something.

"*Sweets to the sweet*," I quoted, handing him a bag of apples. I'd grown up with him testing me on literature by quoting passages and asking me what book they were from. Sometimes he'd reward me with Hershey's Kisses.

"To thine own self be true," he said, pointing at me. I rolled my eyes.

"I'll get right on that."

After we put the groceries away, dad started making dinner and I went to do my homework in the den. This was one of those times when I was happy that it was just the two of us. My mom had left us when I was a toddler, and my older brother Gabe was off at Columbia studying journalism. I missed him like crazy, but we talked at least a few times a week and he texted Dad nearly every day.

I worked steadily, hitting my least favorite subjects first and leaving my English reading for last. Dad was still pissed that I hadn't signed up for AP English, and I didn't think he was going to let it go anytime soon.

"Are you coming to the game?" I asked as I twirled spaghetti on my fork.

"I'm going to try. I have exams to grade, but I'll do my best." He always did. Sometimes he made it to see me cheer and sometimes he didn't, but he tried. He always tried and that was what mattered.

"Have you thought any more about signing up for AP English?" he said and I sighed. I knew it.

"No. I just think that it's not worth it. They don't weigh AP classes, so I can get a perfect grade in regular English. Or I can take AP and have my GPA potentially take a dip. I don't want to do that." Now he was the one to sigh and I was treated to another lecture on the fact that I could gain college credit for taking and doing well on the AP test and blah, blah, blah.

He put down his fork and gave me a long look. Fortunately, I'd gotten most of my looks from him including hair color, eye color and shape, and our mouths did the same thing when we were trying not to smile.

"What if I told you I would give you some money so you could trade in your car and get a nicer one." Shit. He'd picked the *one thing* that I would go for. My car wasn't exactly a piece of crap, but it wasn't really nice either.

I glared at him and he narrowed his eyes and glared back.

"Fine," I said through gritted teeth. "I'll sign up for AP English."

We watched TV together; we always liked the same shows, and then I headed to my room. I worked through my nightly stretches and then got in bed.

The lights were off, but I closed my eyes. This was the only time I let myself think about it. About how when I thought about kissing, it wasn't a boy I imagined. It was a girl. All sweet curves and soft lips. Sometimes her hair was long, and got in my way, sometimes it was short, the blunt ends tickling my fingers. We'd twist around each other until it was impossible to tell us apart.

The desire rushed through me and I welcomed it. I hadn't, at first. It had always been followed by shame. By guilt. Why was I thinking about girls that way? I'd been twelve and most of my friends were swooning over the boys, but I couldn't seem to feel that way. I tried. I tried so hard. I put posters of boy bands in my room and danced with them and tried to flirt with them, but it was just . . . wrong. I didn't like it.

I dated boys here and there, but never went further than that. They would try and I would slam a door in their face. Eventually they lost interest and moved on. I'd given up on that charade a while ago. I was who I was and no boy was going to change that.

I couldn't imagine telling my father and my brother, at least not yet. I would have to someday, obviously, when I got into a relationship. They weren't homophobic, or at least they had never said anything overt, but I didn't want to test them either. Things were fine right now and soon I'd be off to college and I could go all in with whomever I wanted. I'd set that goal for myself and I was going to stick to it.

The last thought I had before I fell asleep was of kissing a set of sweet pink lips.

CHAPTER 2

I was distracted the next day and I wanted to pretend I didn't know why I was distracted but I totally did.

"What is wrong with you today?" Grace asked when I nearly knocked her can of soda off the table at lunch.

"Sorry. Just . . . thinking about stuff." I didn't sound convincing at all. Even to myself.

"Okayyyyy," Grace said, drawing the word out. "You've been weird all day. What's up?" I gave her a look.

"Really? Whenever you have an off day and I ask you what's wrong, you lie to me and now you expect me to talk to you?" She scowled.

"Ugh, whatever. Just be all weird and grumpy. See if I care." She turned away from me to talk to Molly about something.

I tapped her on the shoulder a few minutes later.

"What?" she snapped. You couldn't be sensitive and also be friends with Grace. She could be prickly, but she still had my back and if I needed to hide a body, she would be the one I would call.

"Sorry, I just have a lot on my mind. I had this . . . crazy dream last night and it's been throwing me off all day." So that wasn't a huge lie. I had had a dream last night. The kind of dream that left me waking up gasping and turned on. I could feel my face getting red as I told her. Thankfully, Grace couldn't read minds.

I looked away from her and it was like my eyes were drawn to Stella's table. She was there, sitting and laughing with her friends. Her hair was down in curls and she tossed them over her shoulder. Like she was in a fucking shampoo commercial. I felt my face get redder and told myself to stop looking at her. Not only was she a total bitch, she was also a *girl*.

I shouldn't be getting turned on by a girl. I was straight. I'd had crushes on boys plenty of times. Had even dated a few, but decided that there was no point until I got to college. It was a waste of time that I could better use for studying. Besides, my parents had been super strict about it, so it wasn't worth it.

I didn't like girls. I was just . . . whatever.

Grace snapped her fingers in front of my face.

"Are you there?"

"Yeah, sorry. Just thinking." I kept saying the same thing over and over again and Grace was definitely suspicious.

"Uh huh," she said and I knew she wasn't going to drop it, but the bell rang and we had to go. I kept my head down when I walked by Stella's table and was so focused on not looking at her that I smashed right into someone.

"Oh, I'm sorry!" I said, looking up into a set of crystal blue eyes. They narrowed before she rolled them back in her head and flounced off as I gaped after her.

"Who pee in her Cheerios?" Grace said as Stella flounced away. I felt like I couldn't breathe.

"Don't know," I said, shaking my head and starting to walk again, paying more attention to where I was going.

"She's such a bitch," Grace said, winding her arm with mine.

"Yeah," I said.

The rest of the week was similarly weird. It was like Stella kept getting tossed in my path. Or maybe I just had never noticed her as much. Hell, I was noticing her now. I hated how much I was noticing.

How thick and long her eyelashes were. How her hair fell over her shoulder. How delicate and small her hands were. How her voice had a husky, smoky undertone that was . . .

No. I wasn't noticing things about Stella Davis.

Finally, it was Friday and time for the weekend. I could hang out with Grace and the rest of my friends and not notice Stella Davis for two whole days.

I had not counted on the fact that, of course, Stella would be at the football game. She was captain of the cheerleading squad for fuck's sake. She'd be front and center the whole time. It was going to be even more of a chore not to look at her. I was totally up to the challenge, though. I'd spent the last three years ignoring her (for the most part). How hard could it be?

"What are you staring at?" Grace said, nudging my shoulder.

"Hm?" I said, turning to face her. I had *not* been staring at Stella's ponytail. At all.

"Um, I'm watching the game?" I said, wrapping my arms around myself. It was cold tonight and my ass was already numb on the hard metal bleachers. Grace lifted one edge of her blanket and I scooted closer and we snuggled together.

"You know, we should get one of those family-sized Snuggies," she said as we huddled closer to the rest of our friends.

"That isn't a terrible idea," Paige said. Tommy made a grunting noise on the other side of her. He was too busy watching the game to chat.

"Unpopular opinion time," I said, but only loud enough for Grace to hear. The ref blew a whistle on the field and all the players jogged back to their benches for a time out.

"Yeah?" Grace said, watching the huddle.

"I'm not a fan of football," I said. "Shhh, don't tell anyone." I put my finger to my lips and she rolled her eyes.

"Tell me something I don't know." I went to say something else, but she shushed me. Grace did like football, which was one of the other reasons I came to these things. She got all riled up and it was really funny. More often than not, I watched her instead of the game.

Tonight was different. Tonight I was extremely distracted by a certain cheerleader with blonde hair. It was so cold that instead of wearing the skirts they usually wore during basketball season, they had pants on, but those didn't leave much to the imagination either.

God, what the fuck was wrong with me? I looked around to make sure no one had seen me staring and felt my face get hot. Of course no one was paying attention to me, which was a good thing.

How was it possible that you could be in school with someone for nearly four years and then BAM, you can't stop thinking about them or staring at them or wondering about them . . .

It couldn't be due to Stella's awesome personality. She was generally acknowledged to be not very nice. Not that she did anything overtly mean, but she just gave off that "I'm better than you" vibe and walked around like she owned the world.

I shook my head at myself. I wasn't going to think about Stella's personality. It was irrelevant. I forced my eyes back on the players on the field. I had no idea how anyone could tell them apart with all that gear on Sure, they had their names and numbers on their backs, but still.

Of course, the minute I decided to actually pay attention to the game, it was halftime. The band played first, walking in unison over the field, making a few different formations. We all cheered for our friends and then it was time for the cheerleaders to perform.

Great.

"Wanna get some popcorn?" I said in a strangled voice, grabbing Grace's arm.

"Yeah, sure. You okay?" I nodded jerkily.

"Yeah, just hungry and cold." I didn't let myself watch as they started their cheer and got the crowd to yell back at them. Nope. I kept my back turned and stood in line at the concession stand with Grace.

I was so focused on not paying attention to what was happening on the field that after we got our snacks loaded up in our arms, I nearly ran right into Stella.

"Sorry," I said and she just gave me another look. Like I'd done it on purpose.

"What is your problem?" Grace said. She'd been next to me and had seen the whole thing. Fortunately, only a few kernels of popcorn spilled and I had managed to keep my balance. I wasn't normally this bad at bumping into people. It felt like someone was playing a joke on me.

Stella glared at us both for a second. Her makeup was perfectly in place, despite the fact that she'd been cheering for half of the game. But that was normal. She always looked perfect. Even when she was glaring.

"Nothing. I just don't like people getting in my way," she said and then crossed her arms. I kept my eyes on her face, but I could feel my face getting red.

"Well maybe you should watch where you're going and then it won't happen," Grace snapped, shifting the food so she could take my arm to lead me back in the direction of the bleachers. I couldn't make my mouth work and say words. Why couldn't I say words?

Stella Davis had me tongue-tied and I wanted to scream.

Her blue eyes locked on mine and it was one of those moments

17

when everything goes quiet and it's like you're the only two people in the world. And then she blinked and rolled her eyes.

"Come on," Grace said, tugging at my arm. I stumbled a step before I could regain my footing. Grace was always nice about not walking too fast for me and she held onto my arm all the way back to the bleachers and we sat back down in front.

We handed out the snacks and then Grace turned to me.

"Okay, what the hell was that? You looked like you were . . ." she trailed off.

"I looked like I was what?" A cold drip of fear slid down and pooled into my stomach. I didn't want her to say it at the same time I almost did.

Grace studied my face and then pressed her lips together.

"Never mind," she said, brushing a hand over her hair. It sprung back immediately.

I let it drop. I had been friends with Grace for a long time and I knew her face probably better than my own. I knew what she was going to say without her having to say it.

And it scared the ever-loving shit out of me.

Stella

Was it karma that kept dropping Kyle Blake in my path? That was the second time I'd nearly knocked her over in one week. I felt bad about it, mostly because she had a difficult time walking, but I couldn't bring myself to not be a bitch about everything. If people saw me get soft, things would go back to the way they'd been in middle school and I would die before I let that happen.

So I let her think I was an asshole. I let everyone think that. Hell, I encouraged it. People didn't mess with a bitch. They steered clear of her. They didn't spend their time trying to knock her down and make her suffer. My exterior was steel, topped with razor wire. Come at me and you are going to get cut.

Anyway, I stepped away from her, but not before I got a weird vibe. Like, she was staring at me in a way that she hadn't before. If I didn't know better.

Yeah, no. She was definitely into guys. I'd heard her talk with her friend Grace (another person who didn't take shit from anyone, which I actually admired) about the hot football players and so forth and I was pretty sure she'd had a few boyfriends.

She was kinda cute though. Had that nerdy thing going on with the glasses, and she could do a messy bun that I envied. Ugh, it didn't matter. I wasn't going to go after anyone here. College. Just wait until college.

———◆———

We won the game and afterwards the cheer team went out for pizza. There was a party at Maria's house and since I didn't have anything better to do and the whole squad was going, I went.

It was pretty typical. A bunch of us in the huge basement of her parent's house, some smuggled alcohol, and crappy music. I tried to let go and have a good time, but I couldn't seem to do it.

"What the hell is up with you?" Midori asked me as I sipped a weak wine cooler. I never got plastered at these things because I didn't see the point. Not that I hadn't been wasted before, but the experience had not been enjoyable and I didn't want to repeat it.

I didn't answer as I watched Destiny Cook tangle her tongue with

Brett Forrester's. Gross. I made a face and looked back at Midori. Her brown eyes were studying me in a way I didn't like.

"Nothing," I said, shrugging one shoulder and sitting next to her on the leather couch that had seen better days.

"Yeah, somehow I don't buy that," she said, leaning back. I was saved from having to answer her by a totally bombed Brian Sharpe trying to hit on her and Midori shooting him down. And cursing at him in Japanese until he went away.

She turned her attention back to me and I tried not to squirm under her scrutiny. She'd never said anything about me, never asked, but that didn't mean that she didn't know. I had the sneaking suspicion she did. But she was too much of a good friend to put me on the spot like that.

"So?" she said.

"Just not feeling it tonight. Got a lot on my mind. Dad made me sign up for AP English. I have to start on Monday." I made a face. I had a ton of homework this weekend to catch up on everything I'd missed in the first few weeks of school. It was going to take me several days to get it all done and I wasn't looking forward to it. But I'd suck it up because next weekend Dad was taking me car shopping and I couldn't wait. My car was making a weird grinding noise and I was hoping it would hold out until then.

"That blows." I nodded and she didn't push further. We left early, before things got really out of hand.

"Call me if you need a break or anything," she said when I dropped her off.

"Will do," I said and then headed home. Dad was already in bed, but I went to say goodnight to him.

"Did you witness massive amounts of debauchery?" he asked with a raised eyebrow.

"The usual. It was pretty boring, actually. I'm tired." He kissed my cheek and I went to take a shower before crawling between fresh sheets.

I closed my eyes and sighed. It had been a long day and it was going to be a long weekend. I let my mind wander away from the stress and toward something much more pleasant. Smiles and soft skin and laughter. The stress of the day evaporated and I felt my shoulders relax.

Freedom.

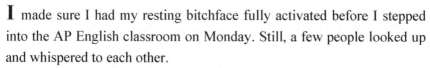

I made sure I had my resting bitchface fully activated before I stepped into the AP English classroom on Monday. Still, a few people looked up and whispered to each other.

"Oh, hello, Stella," Mr. Hurley said. I'd had him my freshman year for English, so at least I didn't have to worry about dealing with a new teacher. I handed him all the makeup work and he gave me a smile. He reminded me a lot of my dad, only he was a few years younger and a little less put together. His glasses were always a little askew and his sweaters usually had at least one hole by the cuffs or the hem.

"Well, you were busy," he said, licking his thumb and then flipping through the pages of essays and handouts I'd nearly killed myself to get done this weekend.

I didn't answer him.

"And you got all the books for this semester?" he asked. I nodded and pulled my copy of *Jane Eyre* out of my bag. It was a worn copy that Dad had given me. I'd read it a few times already. Having an English teacher as a father was a literature class in itself. I'd already devoured most of the required reading list in my younger years and had copies of all of the books at my disposal.

"Great, why don't you take a seat and we'll get started." I turned and looked around. I wasn't friendly with any of the people in this room and as fate would have it, there was only one open seat near the door. Right next to Kyle Blake.

She was doing her best not to look at me, keeping her eyes on the surface of her desk, tracing a pattern with one finger over and over. I heaved a sigh and sat down next to her. She didn't acknowledge me and Mr. Hurley got class started a second later.

"Okay, so we start *Jane Eyre* this week," he said, clapping his hands and rubbing them together as if he'd announced we were going to Disney World. God, he was like my dad. I smiled a little to myself and looked to my left. Kyle had been looking at me. She quickly fixed her eyes back on the front of the class and her cheeks went red.

Weird. I looked back at Mr. Hurley just as he announced that we'd be pairing up to discuss the first three chapters of *Jane Eyre* and filling out a worksheet with our partner. And he pointed to me and Kyle to pair up.

I almost sighed again, but restrained myself. I slowly turned to face her, and she didn't look happy about it either. Mr. Hurley handed out the worksheets and I grabbed it first. Never rely on someone else to do the work in a group project.

"Okay, did you do the reading?" I asked, scanning the questions. They weren't too hard. Just basic information. I could answer all of them by myself, which was good.

"Um, yeah," she said, flipping through her book. The spine was worn and there was some clear tape holding it together. Huh. It was probably one of the school's crappy copies and not a personal copy.

"What are you doing in this class?" she asked as she chewed on her bottom lip and pushed her glasses further up her nose. Had she always had green eyes? I didn't think I'd ever noticed them before. The glasses somehow hid them.

"I transferred," I snapped, starting to work on the first question.

"Hey, what are you writing?" She reached for the paper, but I jerked it away.

"I'm answering the questions. My father is an English teacher. I could do this in my sleep." She gave me a skeptical look and I glared back. This was going so well.

"Well, we're supposed to be doing it together." She waved her hand to indicate the other pairs who had pushed their desks together and

22

were talking.

"Fine," I said, getting up and dragging my desk closer to hers. "Happy?"

For a second I thought she was going to laugh, but she just grabbed the paper out of my hand and put it on her desk, sliding it over so we could both see it.

"There. Okay, so what do you think for the first one?" She bent her head over the paper and I swallowed and leaned closer. I'd never been this close to her and I could just barely smell her perfume. It was like a mix of coconut and vanilla. Like dessert. I tried not to think about it.

She started talking, but I wasn't really listening. I blinked a few times.

"Wait, what?" She gave me a confused look and repeated herself. She pushed her glasses up again and I wondered if it was a nervous habit. They were black plastic frames, but they totally worked for her.

I forced my eyes back on the paper and slowly but surely, we got through the worksheet. I was so relieved when Mr. Hurley asked for us to pass them in and I could move my desk back to where it was supposed to be. But then he made us have a group discussion, which meant moving the desks again into a lopsided circle.

Kyle was having a bit of difficulty getting her desk flipped around so I just grabbed it and did it for her. Instead of getting a "thank you," she looked pissed before slumping into her seat, jaw clenched.

What the hell did I do?

"You're welcome," I said.

"I didn't ask for your help," she said through clenched teeth. I couldn't figure out why she was mad, but I had to admit, she was kinda hot when she was pissed. She had an amazing jawline.

Mr. Hurley cleared his throat and I had to shove my head back into the discussion so I didn't sound like an idiot.

Kyle didn't look in my direction for the rest of class and when it was time to move our desks back, I just went ahead and let her do it, putting my stuff in my bag and leaving without another word.

This class was going to be so much fun.

CHAPTER 3

Seriously. Stella was a straight up bitch. I had only ever had one class with her freshman year; since then we hadn't had much contact, except for last week when we'd kept colliding. Grace was right, though. She was an asshole.

I was still mad about her "helping" me without asking when I met up with Grace for lunch.

"Whoa, you look like you're super pissed. What happened?"

"Stella Lewis is now in my English class. For some reason. No idea how that happened, but she said her dad was an English professor so maybe he pulled some strings for her or something. Basically it means that she's going to be glaring at me and giving me the cold shoulder for the rest of the year," I said, barely taking a breath. I'd been holding onto that rant since I left class.

"Tell me how you really feel, Ky," Grace said, slinging her arm around my shoulder.

"She's just so irritating," I said as we dropped our backpacks at our table and went to get in line for food.

"Uh huh," Grace said, prodding me in the back.

"No I didn't," I said, looking over my shoulder at her. She just smirked and I had no idea what the hell that meant.

"What is happening right now?" I asked as I handed her a tray.

"Oh, nothing, nothing," she said, fiddling around for the silverware. I tried to prod her about it as we got food and then again when we sat down, but she just pretended to zip her lips and refused to talk to me.

I chatted with Molly instead, but I couldn't help but look over at Stella's table. She was sitting with her back to me, her hair draped perfectly over her shoulder. She really was pretty. That kind of easy but polished pretty. And she didn't have to wear a massive amount of makeup to achieve it. The raw materials were all there. I bet she looked amazing with no makeup on.

Yeah, I needed to put a stop to those thoughts like yesterday. I made myself stop looking at her by reminding myself how annoyed I'd been earlier. I just needed to distract myself with something, so I started going through the steps to create different effects in Photoshop. It worked well enough that by the time lunch was over, I had only looked at Stella a few times.

"So, anything new happen today?" my mom asked at dinner and I nearly choked on my asparagus.

"Not really," I said after I sipped some water to clear my throat. I hadn't told them about Stella joining my class because it didn't seem important or relevant.

"You okay?" Dad said, rubbing my back.

"Yup. Just went down the wrong pipe." I changed the subject and then my mom changed it back to my college applications. She'd been into the guidance office at least three times already, begging for applications. They weren't due for months, but she wanted me to "get a jump" on them. Mostly this required me writing tedious essays about my high school experiences and the volunteer work I'd done since I was eleven. It had been mandatory, but I'd enjoyed it. Soup kitchens, building houses, walking shelter dogs, that kind of thing. They wanted me to do it for college, and I just thought it was a nice thing to do. My parents had one-track minds.

I escaped to my room as quick as I could and went back to working on the web design for the blogger. I was so close to being done, I was just doing tweaks and testing to make sure that everything was going to work out and that there weren't any bugs.

I had my headphones on and was blasting Halsey so I didn't hear it when my mom knocked, and I nearly bit m tongue in half when she tapped me on the shoulder.

"Oh my God, Mom, don't do that!" I put my hand on my chest and tried to get my heart to beat at a normal level. She handed me a cup of tea.

"I thought you could use some tea. How's it going?" Um, what? We'd already talked at dinner not that long ago.

"Fineeeee," I said, drawing the word out.

She smiled, but it was one of those placating smiles that parents used right before they dropped bad news.

"Good, good," she said, sitting on my bed. Uh oh. That was the second bad sign.

"Mom, is everything okay?" I asked, knowing I was probably going to regret the answer.

"Oh, fine, fine. Just making sure everything's going to okay. You seemed a bit off at dinner." Shit. My parents were too observant for their own good.

"No, I'm fine. Just busy. Start of the year, you know?" I laughed a little and cringed at how fake it sounded.

Mom patted my arm and I sipped my tea so I wouldn't have to look at her.

"Well, you know that you can talk to your father and me about *anything.*" Okay, this was getting weird. They couldn't possibly know anything about . . .

"Yeah, I know, Mom," I said in a voice that was a little too loud. "I have to get back to work, okay?" I said, pointing at my laptop.

"Sure, honey. Sure." She gave me another smile and put a kiss on the top of my head before leaving and shutting the door quietly behind her.

Um, weird.

Stella

Practice that night was brutal. Everyone was off, even me. I kept having difficulty with my heel stretch, which was nuts because I'd been doing them fine since I was eleven.

Coach ended everything early so there weren't any permanent injuries.

"I don't know what is wrong with all of you, but I hope it's fixed by next practice. None of those stunts should have been falling. You've been doing them for years. Go stretch out and then go home." She walked away, muttering to herself.

I shared a look with Midori.

"Ouch. It's like there's something in the water," she said, stretching her neck out. I got down and started working on my hips and then sunk down into my spits, right, left and middle.

"You okay?" Midori asked as we gathered our stuff and headed out to the parking lot.

"Yeah, just feel off. Maybe it's PMS," I said, even though I knew it wasn't that. She gave me a weird look as we got in the car.

"Are you sure there's nothing you want to talk to me about?" I shook my head.

"Okay, okay. Then will you give *me* some advice?"

"Of course, you don't even have to ask." She took a breath and proceeded to tell me that she had a huge crush on Nate Klein. I had suspected as much, since I'd caught her staring at him during lunch at least ten times in the past two weeks.

"But I don't know if I should go for it. I mean, what's the point? We're just going to end up dating and then breaking up when we go to separate schools. And I'm not in the mood for just a fling." I knew what she meant. Not that I had my eye on anyone. I wasn't dating boys anymore. It sucked and I hated it and I always felt like a liar when I did it. When I first realized that I was attracted to girls, I thought maybe I liked them in addition to boys. And then I'd dated a few boys and realized there was just nothing there for me. But girls? Oh, yeah.

"Well, I guess you have to decide if it's worth the risk. Maybe you won't break up at the end of the year. Maybe you'll stick it out for the long haul. And maybe not." She laughed a little.

"You're so practical sometimes." I guess I was. I never really thought about it much. Sure, romance was fun and wonderful, but it was also work and didn't just happen by magic. Or at least I didn't think it did. To be honest, I didn't think I'd ever really been in love. I'd had feelings for the guys I went out with, but they were only ever friendly. I was just waiting for that one girl to knock me off my feet and then I'd be all in. Just had to get through this last year of high school and then I could go to college and start looking for her.

Kyle was pissy again when I sat next to her on Wednesday.

"This is the only seat in the room, so it's not like I can sit anywhere else," I said, low enough for her to hear, but no one else.

She just made a grumpy sound and I risked a look at her. Cute. She was dangerously cute. I watched as she took down her hair, combed through it with her fingers and then put it up again, exactly the same way. She caught me looking, so I quickly turned and pretended to pay attention to Mr. Hurley, who was going on and on about the paranormal aspects of *Jane Eyre* but I wasn't paying attention. My focus narrowed to one particular point. And she was sitting right next to me, taking notes with her left hand. Had I noticed she was left-handed before? Probably not.

There were a lot of things I discovered about her in that period. Like the fact that she had large, looping handwriting. That she pushed her glasses back up on her nose. A lot. That she had just a few freckles on her nose. There were also several holes in her ears, but only the bottom hole on her lobe had a silver stud in it.

At the end of class, I'd barely taken any notes on the material, but I'd made a hell of a lot of notes about Kyle. This was going to be a continuing problem.

I packed up slowly so we could leave nearly at the same time. I wanted to say something to her, but she just ignored me and kept walking. That made me realize that I couldn't say something to her. I couldn't be friendly toward her. That was *definitely* out of the question. I had to put Kyle Blake out of my mind. Nothing was ever going to happen, so it was crazy to even try.

Yeah, the not-thinking about Kyle lasted until Friday, when I walked into English and realized just how cute she was. How in the hell hadn't I noticed her before this year? She was a neon sign in front of my face and not looking at her was nearly impossible. Somehow she'd flipped a switch and it didn't matter what she did, I was aware of it. I swore I could smell her even after I'd left the room. And at night . . . I thought about taking down her hair and running my fingers through it. It looked soft and smooth. Just the image of wrapping it around my hands was just . . . yeah. I was terrified that she was going to somehow find out that I was thinking about her like that. So my only option was to be ice cold to her. Well, colder than I already was.

That became a problem when Mr. Hurley kept pairing us up to do things in class. Kyle treated me with open disdain, which made being attracted to her even harder than it already was. I had come to the realization that glasses made any girl about five thousand times hotter than she already was. And Kyle had all the raw material. She barely wore any makeup, but I liked that. Sloppy sexy.

"What is your problem?" she hissed at me when she caught me staring.

"Nothing," I said, keeping my tone cool. "Just wondering if you actually read these chapters, or just skimmed Cliff's Notes online." It usually gave me no qualms being like this with most people because the alternative was getting hurt again. I would do whatever it took to not go back there. But I did have a twinge of guilt for being snappy toward Kyle. Didn't stop me from doing it, but it did make me hesitate a little.

"Yes, I did read the chapters," she fired back and grabbed the paper from me. "God, why are you like this?"

I shrugged one shoulder.

"Because."

Her jaw got all clenchy and pretty and I wanted to run my finger along her cheek.

"I get it, I get it. You think you're better than everyone." She rolled her eyes.

"I don't," I blurted out before I could stop myself. Shit. I tried to slam my bitchface back on, but she'd caught me. Her eyebrows flew up and she narrowed her eyes as she looked at me.

31

"You don't?"

I cleared my throat and grabbed the paper back from her, trying to think how to change the subject.

"Hey," she said, her voice so soft that I couldn't ignore it. I shut my eyes so I couldn't see the way she was looking at me. If I did, I didn't think I'd be able to deal with it. What was wrong with me? I'd barely spent any time with her at all. She was an easy target for a crush, that was all. She was new(ish) and she was here. It was opportunity. And she was cute. Nothing more. Hell, I didn't know anything about her, other than what I could observe. I didn't know what she ate for breakfast or if she was a morning person, or what she wanted to do when she graduated. That was what made a crush. This was . . . nothing. It was nothing.

I opened my eyes and narrowed them.

"Let's just get this done," I said. Instead of reeling back, she gave me what was almost a smirk. As if she knew she'd gotten under the surface that I glossed on for everyone else. I was going to have to work twice as hard now to undo that. Great. Just fantastic.

Interesting. Very interesting. Not that I really cared about Stella, but I could have sworn she had a moment of humanity. I didn't know it was possible. That meant one of two things. Either it was a fluke, or it was a moment of weakness. I'd never considered the fact that she might not be a total asshole. The only question was, if asshole wasn't her default setting, then why did she do it?

I guess I could understand a little. I mean, she was captain of the cheerleading team and she hung out with the so-called popular crowd and seemingly had everything. I wouldn't be surprised if she was in the running for prom queen. If it was fake, it was obvious that it had worked for her.

I shook my head at myself. I was thinking way too much about this. She was definitely just a horrible person and would continue to be so. Such a shame because she was definitely pretty. So, so pretty.

———————————◆———————————

"Ungh," Grace moaned on Saturday. We were hanging out at her house, stuffing our faces with pizza and garlic knots and marathoning *Faking It*. I didn't want to watch it, but Grace did, so I'd caved. The thing that made me not want to watch it was the fact that the two main characters were pretending to be a lesbian couple to get popular at their liberal high school. I had to look away every time they kissed. I hated the way it made me feel. Not bad. Good. *Really* good.

What the crap was happening to me? It was like I'd flipped some sort of switch and now all I could do was notice girls in a way I had never thought to notice them before.

"Hey, I forgot to ask, how's class going with Stella?" Grace said. I hadn't been thinking of Stella up until that moment, but the instant Grace said her name, I couldn't get her out of my head.

I laughed nervously. Great.

"She's still the worst," I said, and Grace was preoccupied by the show and didn't see how weird I was being.

"I think she's one of those girls who will always be terrible, but good things will continue to happen for her. Like, she's blessed or something," Grace said. She was blessed all right.

UGH. I needed to stop having those thoughts. But how did you stop your brain from thinking? Other than doing permanent damage.

"Yeah," I said, and got up to stretch.

Grace looked up at me from her position on the floor.

"You sure you're okay?" she asked.

"Yup. Just going to get another soda," I said. "You want anything?" She shook her head and I headed to the kitchen. Her house was quiet since her mom was at the hospital where she worked as an ER doctor and her dad barely left his law practice. Another reason we hung out at Grace's a lot was that her house was five thousand times nicer than mine. It was also about three times the size.

I pulled a Coke out of the fridge and leaned on the marble countertop of the kitchen island for a minute. When I was little, I used to be terrified to make a mess in such a pristine house, but now I was more comfortable. It still didn't feel like a home, more like a movie set, but Grace's room was cozy and comfortably messy.

What was going on with me? I mean, I thought I knew, but that was impossible. I mean, I was straight. Always had been. I'd had plenty of crushes on boys and wanted to get married and all that stuff. I mean, not right now, but in the future. He'd be nerdy and sweet. We'd watch a lot of Doctor Who and maybe cosplay and he'd work for a lab or something.

I had it all planned out. That was what was going to happen. It was what had to happen.

This whole thing with Stella was just a distraction. I was just . . . I don't know.

I peeled myself off the counter and went back to Grace's room. She was laughing her ass off when I got there and pulled me back down to the floor to fill me in on what I'd missed in the show. But my mind was still reeling and my stomach churned as I sipped my soda. The churning had nothing to do with the carbonation.

I was a big fan of research. If I didn't absolutely know everything about a subject, I was determined to learn. So when I got home on Sunday after crashing at Grace's, I locked myself in my room, pulled out my laptop and opened a search engine. I had to figure this out.

My fingers shook at little as they hovered over the keys.

I typed in a few letters, erased them, typed again, erased them. That went on for at least ten minutes until I finally typed in *how do I know if I like girls?* and hit Enter.

And then clicked out of the window before I got any results.

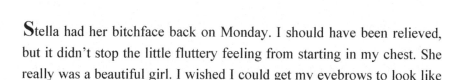

Stella had her bitchface back on Monday. I should have been relieved, but it didn't stop the little fluttery feeling from starting in my chest. She really was a beautiful girl. I wished I could get my eyebrows to look like that.

But her personality was horrible, which was fair. No one should be both gorgeous and have a stunning personality. I was just praying that we didn't get assigned to work together. Fortunately, Mr. Hurley had us read passages aloud, starting with me and going down the rows and back up. I hated reading out loud, but I suffered my way through it. I snickered to myself when a few of the other kids in the class stumbled over some of the more difficult words.

And then it got to Stella and I riveted my eyes on my desk, so I wouldn't look at her. She started to read and for some reason, her voice got all low and melodic and holy *shit*. She didn't stumble on any of the words and didn't read it in the same robotic voice as everyone else. She read as if she was on stage, doing a dramatic recitation and I looked up to see if anyone else was being affected by it like I was.

A cursory glance around the room said no. I felt my face going red and I looked back at my desk. She finally finished and sat down. I breathed a sigh of relief.

Out of the corner of my eye, I saw her look over at me. I wasn't going to turn my head because then we'd make eye contact and I just couldn't.

English class had never been fraught with so much tension ever in my life and I just wanted it to be over.

There were several feet of space between me and Stella, but I wished there were miles. I just couldn't NOT be aware of her. Every time she touched her hair, or moved her legs, or breathed, I was aware of it. She had skinny jeans on that hugged and accentuated everything, a filmy top that I could never pull off, and cute little ballet flats. As always, her hair was perfect.

I wanted to run away, but class was almost over. I made a frustrated sound that was louder than I thought it was. Finally, I turned and saw Stella giving me a puzzled look. I just wanted to grab her snotty, stuck up face and . . .

I raised my hand and asked to go to the bathroom. Mr. Hurley let me go and I nearly knocked my desk over in my haste to leave the room. I nearly fell when I got through the door because my brain was moving faster than my feet, but I caught myself on the wall and headed toward the bathroom. I didn't care how it looked; I was camping out in there until English was over.

It was only ten minutes. I could do it.

I had about two minutes left before the bell rang when someone came through the door. I had sequestered myself in the last stall, hoping that no one would notice that I was standing.

I waited for them to pick one of the other stalls, do their thing and leave, but the footsteps just kept advancing until the person was right near my stall. I wondered if I should flush or something, but then whoever it was spoke.

"Kyle?"

CHAPTER 4

Stella

I don't know what made me do it. But she looked so freaked out and she'd hurried so fast to get out of class that I couldn't just sit there. What if she was sick and needed help?

Okay, that was a flimsy excuse, but it didn't stop me from asking Mr. Hurley if I could run to the office for something. If someone else had asked, he probably would have said no, but he liked me too much and went ahead and let me go.

I figured she'd gone for the bathroom, so I headed that way and saw her black Chucks under the door of the last stall. I didn't hear anything but her breathing, so I decided to risk it.

"Kyle?" Silence. "Are you okay?" She coughed and the toilet flushed before she pushed through the door. Her face was totally red and I wondered what the hell I was doing. Why had I followed her in here like a total stalker?

I needed to turn around and run away. There was no easy way to salvage this situation.

"I'm fine," she said, and it sounded like those two words should end with a question mark. "Why are you in here?"

I opened my mouth to answer and then the bell rang. Two seconds later, the door opened and we weren't alone. She pushed past me and headed out the door.

I stood there for a second before a girl gave me a nasty look. I gave her one back and left, heading to my locker.

———————————◗◆◖———————————

My dad had kept his word about the car, so on Saturday he'd taken me shopping and I was now the owner of a new-to-me vehicle.

"Not bad," Midori said when she got in after practice. It had a lot of upgrades over my old wheels, namely the leather interior and Bluetooth capability. I'd already synched all my music, which was awesome.

"Not at all," I said.

"So," she said, taking down her ponytail and combing her fingers through her hair. "Everything okay? You were a little out of it today." I knew she'd noticed. After the weirdness with Kyle, I was off the rest of the day. I forgot to be so much of an asshole and got some strange looks from my friends when I wasn't at my normal level of icy composure.

I was able to throw myself into practice because we were working on heel stretch double downs and I had to focus or else I would seriously hurt someone.

"Yeah, fine. Why?" I switched the songs to have something to do.

"Don't know. You just seemed . . . off." I flipped through songs until Midori put her hand on mine to make me stop.

"Stel." I looked at her and then back at the road.

"I'm fine. I just don't want to talk, okay? I just . . ." I gripped the steering wheel. I knew Midori wouldn't care about me liking girls. I knew it wouldn't change anything. But actually saying the words out loud and telling her was something I just couldn't do. Not yet. College. I would be who I wanted to be in college. It just wasn't the right time. I wasn't ready.

"It's fine, it's fine. Don't worry about it." She pulled back and I was so grateful. The pressure to tell her weighed on me, but it was a weight I could deal with. I'd been handling it for years.

So why did it suddenly feel like it was crushing me?

———————◆◆———————

"**H**ow's the car?" Dad asked when I got home. He had dinner ready, but I wasn't that hungry.

"Great. The heated seats are going to be a bonus in the winter." He smiled at me and we chatted about this and that for a few minutes, but then my phone rang and it was my brother. I answered at the table.

"Hey, Gabe," I said.

"Hey, Star. How's life?" My brother was the most upbeat member of my family. And I was a cheerleader.

"Good, how's school? You failing yet?" He laughed.

"Hell no. Dean's list, Sis." I rolled my eyes. Stupid smart family full of overachievers.

"You would. Are you having any fun?"

"Here and there. Not the kind of fun you're thinking of. I don't think passing out on the sidewalk naked and being found by campus security is my idea of a good time." I agreed and we talked more about his classes and campus life. He was so lucky to be in New York and surrounded by so much culture and life and diversity. I couldn't wait to get the hell out of Maine.

Dad motioned for the phone and I handed it over so he and Gabe could chat about his assignments and his recent articles he'd had published. I knew that was going to take a while, so I took our plates and rinsed them in the sink.

After Dad was done, I took the phone and headed into my room so I could talk to Gabe without Dad overhearing.

"Okay, so tell me what you're really up to now that I'm not sitting next to Dad," I said, flopping on my bed.

"Nothing. I told you, I've been a good boy. I honestly don't have time to get shitfaced with all the work I'm doing in class and on the paper and freelancing. You'll understand when you get to college next year. It's so much more work than people say it is." I could believe that, but I could also believe that Gabe was taking on too much. He always did. If he wasn't careful, he was going to run himself into the ground before he turned thirty.

"Have you even been on a date?" I asked. I would much rather grill my brother about his love life than talk about mine. Or lack thereof.

"Not really. I've been doing the casual sex thing."

"Ugh, TMI, Gabe. TMI!" I wished I could throw a pillow or something at him. He just laughed again.

"I'm kidding. Sort of. Sometimes this girl from one of my study groups comes over, but usually we're so tired that we just pass out before we can even get to the sex. I figure I'll get to have sex when I graduate." I rolled my eyes at him, but he couldn't see.

"How's your love life? Any developments there? Still sticking to the 'no dating until college' rule?"

"Yes, I am." I didn't sound sure. Oh, hell.

"Is that some hesitation I hear in your voice? Did you meet someone?" He didn't specify a gender. We hadn't for a long time. But I still hadn't told him that I wanted to date girls.

"No. Definitely not." I didn't sound sure about that either. But just as I thought he was going to start interrogating me, I heard someone call his name.

"Shit, listen. I have to go, but we need to have a longer talk soon. Oh, and when are you coming to visit?" I always flew down to see him at least a few times a year on our school breaks. He took me around the city and we went shopping and he let me see what it was going to be like to be a college student. I couldn't wait to get back.

"I can't remember the exact day our break starts on, but I'll text you." We said goodbye and hung up. I was actually relieved that I didn't have to talk to him anymore.

Gabe was perceptive as hell and I was ninety percent sure he already knew. Once again, saying the words just seemed impossible. For the millionth time in my life, I wished I just liked boys. I'd tried. Sometimes I still tried. I'd look at a popular male actor or model and ask myself if I found him attractive.

Nope. Nothing. Absolutely nothing. It was like looking at marble sculpture. Pleasing to the eye, but I didn't want to buy it.

Kyle still floated in the back of my head. She'd been lurking there all day in all her adorable glory. She really was cute as hell. I was an idiot for ignoring it so long. Now I couldn't see anything else.

She had definitely looked freaked out in the bathroom today, but that was probably because she hadn't expected me to come and find her. I groaned and rolled over onto my stomach. I was such an idiot. Why had I done that? Things were going to be so awkward on Wednesday when I saw her again.

I turned back over and put my hands behind my bed as I stared up at the ceiling.

I was just going to go back to avoiding her. It would be easy. Totally easy. Impossibly easy.

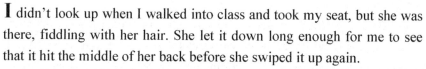

I didn't look up when I walked into class and took my seat, but she was there, fiddling with her hair. She let it down long enough for me to see that it hit the middle of her back before she swiped it up again.

I'd considered saying something, or apologizing about the bathroom weirdness, but my instinct told me to just let it go and pretend it hadn't happened.

And then, in his infinite wisdom, Mr. Hurley said the words that every student dreaded, "Okay, pair up." I searched around the room, but in the seconds after he'd spoken, the pairs had already formed, as if they'd just been waiting for this moment. There was the sound of desks sliding and people moving seats and then it was just me and Kyle.

I looked at her and she looked at me and it was inevitable.

"Guess I have no choice," I said, trying to sound bored while my heart was beating roughly three thousand miles a minute.

"Yup," she said, sounding irritated. Mr. Hurley handed out our assignments. Great. We had to pick from a list of topics, write a three page paper together and do a presentation for the rest of the class. We were going to have to work together for the next two weeks.

Oh, hell.

I was really beginning to hate Mr. Hurley. Did he understand how horrible it was to make you work with someone you didn't want to work with? Hadn't he been in school once? Maybe it was too long ago. He was old and had gray hair.

Whatever the reason, I had to look forward to working very closely with Stella for the next two weeks. No way around it. She and I would have to work in-class and outside to get everything done. Great. Just great.

"So . . ." she said, grabbing the topic list before I could reach for it. "I think we should do the one about feminism. Because *Jane Eyre*'s clearly a feminist text." I hadn't even seen the choices and I wanted to smack her because that did sound awesome.

"Do I get a say, or are you just going to do the entire thing yourself?" I said, my tone dry. She raised one absolutely perfect eyebrow and handed me the paper. I scanned the topics and I could feel her studying me. I pushed my glasses back up my nose and looked at her. I hadn't really absorbed what the paper said and I couldn't tell her that.

"Fine, we can do the feminism thing. But I want to write the paper. I type really fast." She gave me another eyebrow raise and I tried to do it too, but failed. My eyebrows weren't that coordinated.

Something passed over her face and she slid her eyes back down to the paper.

"Fine. But I get to do the presentation."

"Fine." I was absolutely fine with that. She was much more of a performer than I was, with the cheerleading and all. I'd probably end up stumbling over my words and messing it up. Stella probably knew that too.

There was a moment where neither of us knew what to say. The quiet hum of talk seemed distant. It almost felt like the two of us were completely alone. And then Mr. Hurley walked over and cleared his throat.

"Better get started, ladies." He gave us a Stern Look and I glanced at Stella. For a brief second, I could have sworn she was holding in a smile. But she smoothed her expression like a wrinkle out of fabric and it was gone.

"Guess we should start," I said to her.

"Guess we should."

The rest of the class we spent in terse conversation. I was in charge of pulling quotes from the book we could use in our paper and Stella was busy looking up other sources on one of the classroom tablets.

For the most part, we could work quietly, but when we did have to exchange a few words, it was short and to the point.

Still, I couldn't take my eyes off her. As if it was planned that way, a shaft of sunlight broke through one of the windows and lit her hair on fire. If I didn't know better, I would have said she looked like an angel. And then she turned and gave me a look and I edited my assessment. Fallen angel. Fallen angel that was kinda bitter about the whole thing.

It was just then that I realized I'd been staring. Dammit.

I shoved my face in my book and tried to get back to work. A moment later I looked up because she'd cleared her throat.

"What do you think about this?" Her voice was softer than I'd ever heard it and I nearly fell out of my seat when she leaned over with the tablet to show me whatever was on the screen. I looked down at it, but it could have been written in emojis for all I noticed. She was too close. Way too close and I was freaking out about it. My heart was pounding so much that I was sure she could hear it and my hands suddenly went cold and then hot.

"Well?" she said, her voice totally breathy and low. I turned my head just a fraction and whoa.

Her eyes were crazy gorgeous up close. They weren't just blue. They had little flecks of green, right around the center. Like emeralds in a pool of water. She blinked the longest lashes I'd ever seen on a real person and suddenly breathing became a chore.

A rush of heat started from the top of my head and poured down my body into my toes. I had never felt this way before and it didn't seem to be going away. Stella stared at me, lips slightly parted and then jerked back, as if I'd punched her.

"Stop staring at me," she snapped, putting her icy face back on. I blinked a few times and it was like coming up for air after being underwater. I was gasping and disoriented.

I coughed once and then sat back. I'd leaned way far over without realizing it. Stella didn't appear affected at all.

Except.

Except for the slightest tremor in her hand as she held the tablet.

Huh.

———————◆———————

"So I think we should get a head start on everyone else," she said briskly, just before class ended. We'd made good headway on our project, but I had the feeling Stella wasn't going to be satisfied unless it was absolutely and totally perfect.

"What do you mean?" I asked, knowing the answer wasn't going to be good.

"I think we should get the paper done by the end of this week so we can perfect the presentation. As much as I hate to say it, I think we should get together outside of class and work." She made a face like the idea disgusted her, but I wasn't buying it. I'd seen a few cracks in her shiny surface and I was just waiting to see more. People were right when they said Stella was like ice. An iceberg was a little more accurate. There was something below the surface that no one had seen before. I didn't know what made me want to figure her out, but I did. I wanted it a lot.

"Okay," I said, a little too quickly. I shouldn't have been so eager.

"We'll have to do it later because I have practice. And at one of our houses because the library will be closed." Great. Just what I needed.

"Not my house," I said, my voice too loud. "My parents are insane and will drive both of us crazy." She gave me a look and then said, "Fine. My house."

"I mean, really. They're like the textbook definition of helicopter parents." Why was I still rambling? She just sighed and looked toward the door as if she wanted to escape.

"It's fine. Seriously. Look, I have to go." Her eyes snapped back to me and then she lunged out and grabbed my phone from where it rested on the corner of my desk. Before I could protest, she handed it back.

"There. I'll text you when practice is over and give you directions. You'd better be there on time and ready to work." With that, she got to her feet, threw her hair over her shoulder and was out the door.

Ice storm Stella strikes again.

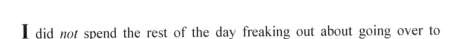

I did *not* spend the rest of the day freaking out about going over to Stella's.

Okay, that's a lie. I did.

"I bet her house is all white and you can't sit on the furniture," Grace said, which was a little funny, considering the house she lived in. But she was trying to be supportive.

"I have no idea. It's going to be beyond awkward. My plan is to get in and get out as fast as possible." With hopefully my dignity and sanity intact. It was definitely going to be harder to stop staring at her and being weird if it was just the two of us. If she suggested we do this in her room, I was going to veto that. I didn't want to be anywhere in her personal space. For some reason.

"Well, you can always text me and I'll come rescue you with some sort of emergency." Grace was that kind of best friend who would fake a life-threatening emergency to get you out of an awkward situation. She'd done it many times before with great success.

"Thanks, I might take you up on that," I said as we headed to our cars.

CHAPTER 5

Stella

I wasn't nervous. Not at all. I wasn't fidgeting and re-arranging the shakers on the dining table and then going to the fridge to make sure we had enough soda and then checking the couch to make sure there were no dust bunnies underneath.

Nope. I wasn't doing any of those things.

I'd booked it out of practice so I could get home and get a shower in (and redo my hair) before she came over. I sent the text with shaking fingers. I almost wished that Dad was home to distract me, but he was working late tonight so it was going to be just me and Kyle.

Bad idea.

Such a bad idea.

I'd regretted the words almost the instant they were out of my mouth, but there was no way to pull them back so here I was, fiddling with my hair and waiting for her to show up. I drew the line at waiting by the door.

Finally, what seemed like hours later, a car pulled into the driveway. God help me.

I was able to pretend that I totally didn't care that she was here, in my house with me, alone. She'd changed into low-slung grey sweatpants that left just a hint of belly showing under her t-shirt. Just that little whisper of skin was enough to make my mouth go dry and I had to remind myself to look up at her face, but that was somehow worse.

The lighting in my house must have been designed to make her look as cute as possible or else I was just imagining things. I narrowed my eyes and led her to the dining room table where I had my laptop set up and my book out already, with passages I'd highlighted. I'd needed something to do while I was waiting for her.

"Do you want anything?" I said, trying to sound bored as I went to the kitchen.

"Um, Coke? If you have it." Her eyes kept darting around, as if looking for a neon sign to point her toward the emergency exit. I was feeling a little that way myself.

I grabbed two cans and two glasses and nearly dropped everything when she got up to help me.

"I've got it," I snapped and she put her hands up and backed away.

"Sorry, sorry. Just trying to be nice, no need to bite my head off." I'd like to bite her, but not in the way she was thinking.

I could feel my face starting to flush, so I got busy pouring out the sodas and then asking her if she wanted a snack. She declined, but I was still starving from practice, so I grabbed a few bags of chips and some berries from the fridge.

Kyle gave me a look when I set them down between us.

"The chips and the berries cancel each other out. It's basic food science," I said and I swore she almost smiled. Almost.

"I'm pretty sure that's not how calories work, Stella." Wow. I really liked the way my name sounded in her mouth.

Stop thinking about her mouth.

Hard to do when she scooped up a handful of berries and started popping them in said mouth.

I was going to die. This girl was going to kill me.

I cleared my throat and put my laptop screen in front of me so it blocked the view.

"So, I pulled a few passages already, if you want to look at them and then copy them down for the paper. I could also have my dad go over it before we hand it in," I said. He'd already been doing that for every paper I'd ever written. It was a habit that I didn't intend on breaking.

She raised her eyebrows and there was a smudge of berry juice in the corner of her mouth. I stomped on a mental image of leaning forward to lick it off.

"Yeah? You're going to give it to your dad and he's going to rip it apart and then you're going to have him fix it and hand it in anyway," she said, crossing her arms.

"No, he's going to tell us where it's weak and where it's good and make sure that the grammar is correct," I said, keeping my eyes on my laptop. I was pretending to type, but really, I was just pressing random keys.

"Or, stay with me here, you're going to re-write the entire paper, slap our names on it and then hand it in. I get it, you're a control freak." My mouth almost dropped open and I risked a look up to stare at her.

"What the hell are you talking about?" I'd been called worse before, but for some reason this really got under my skin.

"Uh, is this new information? Like, are you really surprised?" Her voice was totally dry and I wished I was less attracted to her because that would make things so much easier.

"I'm not a control freak, I just like things a certain way." She let out the cutest little snort-laugh and it did funny things to my stomach. Was there anything she did that didn't make me want her more?

"That's a diplomatic way of putting it, babe," she said and then we both realized she'd called me "babe."

Oh. Hell.

We just sort of stared at each other and then she cleared her throat and looked down at her book.

"So we should probably get to work," she said in a low voice.

"Yeah."

Nearly an hour later, we'd demolished the berries, one bag of chips, three sodas between us and we hadn't gotten much done. It wasn't for lack of trying. We just didn't see eye-to-eye on the paper.

"This was such a bad idea," she said as she typed in the Google Doc that I was also working on at the same time. "You just keep deleting everything!"

I hadn't been. Just editing here and there. Picking a better word or making a sentence stronger or adding a comma. Nothing major. But she saw it as an assault against her writing skills, which were actually better than I thought they would be.

Not that I doubted her ability to write, but I just thought that numbers were more her speed, but she had some excellent points and used a lot of words that I didn't know she knew.

She was smart. Really smart.

If only she'd been pretty and dumb, I might have been able to resist her. But the smart/sexy combo? I was a goner.

"I like to think of it more as polishing what's already there and making it shine," I said.

"You always have the most diplomatic way of putting things. Makes me wonder where all those rumors come from." She tried to make it a throwaway comment, but it definitely wasn't.

"What rumors?" I asked, as if I had no idea. Hell, I started a lot of them myself. Had to keep reminding people not to mess with me.

"I'm sure you're familiar with them, Stella."

"Why would I be?" I asked, trying to sound oblivious.

She just rolled her eyes at me. Cute. So cute.

"You also don't seem like an idiot, so let's cut the crap, okay? You know exactly what people say about you. I wouldn't be shocked if you were the one who encouraged it."

No. This was bad. This was why I didn't let people get too close. Midori was one of my exceptions. When people got close they could see me clearly and I didn't like it. If they really saw me, they wouldn't like me.

I just narrowed my eyes at her and didn't answer. Most people looked away from me after a few seconds, but Kyle held my gaze and then one side of her mouth turned up in a smirk. The smirkiest of smirks.

"You get quiet when you don't know what to say. Means I'm right."

There wasn't much I could say without digging myself an even bigger hole, so I just turned my attention back to my laptop and thought about highlighting the entire paper and deleting it like a bitch, but then I'd have to spend even more time with her and that wouldn't be good for anyone.

"I think that's enough," I said after a few minutes of silence. I had to get her out of here. She was all I could see and all I could hear and all I could smell and it was a real problem. I had to get her out of here before I did something stupid.

She took off her glasses and rubbed her eyes before putting them back on. I still had a bunch of other homework to do and I was sore from practice.

She looked at me and then down at her laptop.

"Yeah, I guess." Was she reluctant to leave? After all the stimulating conversation?

"What, you want to stay and hang out with me?" I injected just the right amount of acid into each word.

"It's better than being at home," she muttered, as if she didn't want to admit it.

"Are you parents really that bad?" I asked before I could stop myself.

"Not really. I mean, it's that they *care* too much. How can you be pissed that your parents care too much about you and want you to succeed? What kind of asshole am I?" I wasn't going to answer that right away.

"I'm sure there are plenty of people who wish they had two parents who aggressively cared about them," I said. I hadn't been speaking specifically about me, but I guess I did fit the bill. My mom had cared about me long enough to give birth to my brother and then me, but had decided that being a mom just wasn't for her. You know, she couldn't have figured that out until after she'd gotten married and had us.

"That's right, make me sound like an ungrateful bitch. Perfect. Way to go, Stella," she said, grabbing her stuff and heading toward the door. I wanted to go after her and tell her that she was the opposite of a bitch, but then that might have led to all sorts of other things, so I let her go, calling "bye," after her.

Seriously. What a fucking bitch. Her personality was just that terrible. I'd been wrong. Maybe the glimpses of nice I'd seen were an act. Who the hell knew?

I was fuming when I got home and that made my parents go into a panic and have another one of their little "interventions" with me. Any time I showed any sort of excessive negative emotions, they sat me down and had a "chat."

I wanted to tell them that I was fine, just annoyed. That I wasn't secretly depressed, or cutting my wrists, or hiding an eating disorder. In addition to being human helicopters, they were also hyper-hypochondriacs. Everything had the potential to be life-threatening, from a cold to a slammed door. When I was younger I used to wish at every birthday and every Christmas that I would get a sibling that they could focus on. Never happened and I was pretty sure that ship had sailed a long time ago.

Once I got them off my back and assured them that I was not going to hurt myself or anyone else, I barricaded myself in my room to fume.

I didn't know why she drove me so crazy. Just . . . everything she said and did just . . .

Fuck.

I could pretend the little fluttery feeling in my chest wasn't there, but that wouldn't make it go away. I . . . liked her. Or something.

I didn't know why. I didn't know when it had started, but there it was. I liked her in a way that made me wonder how soft her lips would feel and if her hair was silky to the touch. It made me think of lots of other things too. Things that made me want to get in the shower and spend some time alone.

Dangerous. Those were very dangerous thoughts that I should not be having, but there really wasn't any way to stop them. They were happening and I had to just get through it. I was stuck with Stella for the foreseeable future, unless I dropped out of AP English, but that wasn't an option.

I'd just have to keep a lid on it. Keep it to myself. It was just a little crush (I hated even calling it that) and I could handle it. I was a nearly grown-ass woman and I could deal with a tiny crush on a terrible girl.

I could deal.

———————◆———————

It didn't hurt that she was so cold. If she'd been nice to me, I might have liked her more. Or maybe not. Verbally sparring with her was kind of sexy.

Fuck, fuck, fuck.

Somehow the two of us got through the week without killing one another and I managed to not do anything that would have let her know how I felt. She pulled back a lot, but wasn't as critical. She'd press her lips together and I knew she was trying not to say something she wanted to say.

Friday night was another home game and I was there on the bleachers in the front row with Grace. And there was Stella, her hair up high and a smile on her face. It was a little funny that she was so frigid most of the time, but chose a sport like cheerleading to excel in.

And holy shit, did she excel. Flips and stunts and all kinds of stuff that made me think about all kinds of things. My face was probably beet red the entire game, but I couldn't take my eyes off her.

Fortunately, she seemed oblivious of me. Except for one moment when she was front and center, leading a cheer where the crowd had to respond. Her blue eyes seared into me for one moment and then slid back to scan the rest of the crowd.

Fuck with a side of fuck.

Grace didn't say much during the game, and I realized she was upset about something. Her eyebrows were drawn together in a constant frown and I decided that I had to get my head out of my own ass and be a best friend.

"You okay?" I asked, touching her arm when we went to get sodas at halftime.

"Yeah, sure," she said, totally unconvincing.

"I'm sorry I've been distracted. What's up with you?" I turned her to face me and she wouldn't look at me. Yup, something was definitely bothering her.

"It's my parents. They're being stupid about college. They want me to get a 'sensible' degree." She used her fingers to put air quotes around sensible.

"And what does that mean?" She sighed and rubbed her hand through her hair.

"I don't know, business or something? Pre-law? Pre-med? Anything with the word 'pre' in it? Not art or music or anything like that. And don't even get them started on journalism or graphic design." Now this, I could relate to.

"You've met my parents, right? They're going to flip their shit if I don't get a PhD in something fancy and have a six-figure starting salary." Not because they wanted me to be rich, but because they wanted me to be *secure*. Their word, not mine. I had no idea what the hell I wanted to do, and that was a serious problem for them.

"Yeah, I know. It just sucks when I think they're going to let me do what I want, but then lay down the hammer. They're saying that they'll only pay for school if I major in something they approve." Well. That sucked. My parents didn't have a whole lot of money to send me to college, so I was going to have to rely on a lot of scholarships, which was one of the reasons I took so many AP classes and had taken the SATs four times to get a good enough score to qualify for more than a few. I was going to be spending a hell of a lot of time writing essays and so forth after I applied. Just my idea of a good time.

"Hey, you still have a lot of time. And do you honestly believe that they won't support you financially if you become an artist? Please. You're going to be amazing at whatever you do, Grace." I slung my arm around her shoulder and she leaned her head against mine.

"You always make things sound easier than they are, but I totally appreciate it," she said.

I heard a throat clear behind us and I turned to find Stella there, with one exquisite eyebrow raised.

"Can I help you in some way?" I said, trying to sound as icy as she did.

"No, you're just holding up the line," she fired back. I had no idea what she was talking about and then I realized Grace and I had been kinda holding up the line.

"Sorry not sorry," I fired at Stella and then moved to the counter to order.

Stella definitely muttered something under her breath, but I didn't quite catch it.

"So I guess she hasn't sweetened any," Grace said as we walked back to the bleachers. Everyone else was deep in conversation about the upcoming Fall Formal, so I let myself be drawn into that conversation.

"Are you going to ask someone?" Grace said, a weird look on her face.

"No, why would I? I haven't had a date to any of the other dances, why start now?" Our group always went together and I didn't see a reason to mess with tradition.

"No reason. But if there was someone you wanted to take, you could, you know."

"I know," I said, slowly.

"Okay," she said, giving me one last look before turning to Paige and asking if she'd gotten her dress yet and if we should plan a shopping trip for the next weekend. I agreed, even though I had a perfectly cute dress already in my closet that I'd bought last summer. I needed a weekend that didn't involve football, Stella, or my parents.

I was twitchy on Saturday and Sunday, constantly checking my phone. I told myself it wasn't because of Stella, but that was a huge lie. I didn't know why I wanted her to text me, because it would probably be something mean anyway. There was no way I was going to text her anything. Not even if my house was on fire.

Still, I typed out a few terrible messages and then deleted them. I cringed at myself and went back to watching re-runs of Buffy.

***

"So, did you finish the edits I suggested?" Stella said to me on Monday. We'd nearly finished, but she still wasn't satisfied. I was beginning to think that nothing ever satisfied Stella Lewis, but that wasn't my problem.

"I did, but I really don't think that comma belongs there," I said. We'd had a comma battle last week that had almost ended in bloodshed. I'd even gone so far as to look it up online and print out a few articles that proved I was right. I had them in my bag, ready to show her.

But then she did something that had me so shocked I almost fell off my chair.

"You're right."

I sputtered for a second.

"I'm sorry, could you repeat that for the people in the back?" I said, cupping my hand to my ear.

She rolled her eyes and then narrowed them.

"You heard me. I'm not going to say it again, so drop it." I couldn't contain the laugh that bubbled out of my mouth.

"You don't like being wrong, do you?" She looked back down at her notebook and turned a page of her notes.

"It doesn't happen very often. I'm nearly always right."

"Wow, you should really work on your self-esteem issues, Stella," I said and she gave a little start when I used her name. I couldn't seem to stop using it whenever I could. It was a pretty name for a pretty girl.

"I can't help it if I'm right. It just happens," she said and I almost caught a smile.

"What a hardship for you," I said, but I realized that we were teasing each other. Holy shit, I was flirting with her.

I was flirting with Stella and she was kinda flirting back.

What the fuck was even happening?

The moment died when she brushed her hair back and turned toward me.

"Now. About the presentation." We were back to business.

———————◆———————

Two days later I was at Stella's house again and she was giving our presentation for an audience of one. Me.

I was trying to keep my mind on what she was saying, but it was hard to focus on that because of the way her mouth moved when she talked. The tone of her voice. The way she stood. It was all . . . sexy. So sexy.

Just a crush. A weird, out of the blue crush on a girl. Everyone had had one of those in their life, right? It didn't mean I was . . . I mean, I still liked guys. I totally liked guys. I totally . . .

Was staring at her boobs.

I was just jealous of them. Mine weren't shaped that nice. That was it. And her shirt was cute. I was not staring at her boobs, imagining what they would look like without the shirt.

Nope. Not even a little bit.

I dragged my eyes back up to her face and found her staring at me expectantly.

"Well? How was it? And keep the editorial comments to a minimum." Oh. She'd finished the presentation and I hadn't even noticed. Because I'd been staring at her boobs.

This was starting to be a serious problem. Thank God our presentation was on Monday and then we wouldn't have time alone together anymore. I couldn't handle it.

"Uhhh, good. Really good," I said, stumbling to come up with something, anything, to say. She sighed and threw up her hands, notecards scattering to the floor.

"You weren't even listening. I can't believe this. You may not care about this class, but I do." Now that made me mad.

"I do care about this class, seeing as how I've been in it since the beginning of the year. Where the hell were you?" I got to my feet and then we were standing about a foot apart, both equally pissed.

"That's irrelevant. I'm in this class now and I don't want to get a shitty grade because I'm stuck working with you."

I took a step forward and we were almost chest-to-chest.

"Oh, I'm so sorry that it's been so *awful* to work with me, you should have just gone to Mr. Hurley asked him to do the whole thing yourself. Oh wait, you pretty much did that anyway!"

Our eyes are locked and I could feel that this was one of those intense moments where the world just stops.

We're both breathing a little too hard for what happened and then Stella did something that shocked me more than if she would have pulled out a gun and shot me.

She kissed me.

CHAPTER 6

Stella

I had no idea what made me do it. Maybe I was hormonal, or hadn't kissed anyone in a long time, or maybe I had been poisoned during lunch and this was some side effect, but one minute she was standing in front of me yelling and the next I had pressed my mouth to hers.

The contact lasted all of a half a second, because she pulled away so fast. I teetered on my toes and nearly lost my balance. I'd been leaning so far into her that I had to grab the back of a chair so I didn't crash to the floor.

"What the fuck, Stella?!" she said, putting her hands up and backing away. "Seriously, what the *fuck?*"

"I'm sorry," I said automatically. "I'm sorry." I had no idea why I was apologizing. I mean, yeah, it probably wasn't the best idea to kiss her, but I'd thought . . .

No, that was impossible.

"I'm sorry," I said again, my voice sounding robotic. She spun around in a circle while ripping the elastic viciously out of her hair. The brown semi-waves tumbled down to her shoulders and she was so cute. So, so cute.

Cute and pissed, but that was a good look for her.

"You just . . . You just kissed me," she said, spinning around. "You just fucking kissed me. What the fuck?" She certainly liked to swear a lot when she was taken off-guard. But I thought her reaction was a little extreme for the situation. I mean, was me kissing her the worst thing that had ever happened to her?

"I don't know," I said. That was the truth. I didn't know. Well, I did. I knew that I thought she was adorable as hell and that I had wanted to kiss her for a while and that it had finally become too much and my body had sort of taken over, but other than that, I had no idea why I specifically liked *her*.

Sure, there was the cute factor and she was smart and sexy and she could be funny when she wanted to, but she wasn't . . . I mean she wasn't, say, Natalie Dormer, who was hot as fuck. She was just Kyle.

I licked my lips and tried to tell myself that I couldn't taste her.

"I have to go. I seriously have to go," she said, grabbing her things and stumbling, dropping her copy of *Jane Eyre* in her haste to get out. Her limp slowed her down a little and I grabbed her arm, reaching down to get the book.

"You don't have to go. I'm sorry. I shouldn't have done it. I don't know what happened." Oh, what a lie.

"This is just . . . so, so fucked up. You're seriously fucked up, Stella." My insides clenched when she said my name. She wrenched her arm away from me.

"Stay away from me." I let her go because what else was I going to do? I couldn't force her to stay and I wasn't going to explain everything and I was still so messed up from the fact that I'd even done it that I just let her walk out the door.

"**H**ow did studying go?" Dad asked an hour later when he came home. He'd been working a lot of extra hours at the college lately, but it made him happy, so I didn't mind. Plus, it had been a blessing in disguise tonight. I didn't know what I would have done if he'd walked in on me kissing Kyle.

I choked on a piece of popcorn and had to chug some water before I could breathe again.

"Fine. We, ah, practiced our presentation so I think we're ready for Friday." I knew my presentation was solid, but now I had this fear that I was going to mess it up due to what happened earlier.

I wanted to groan and bury my head in the couch cushions. I'd definitely messed up and the embarrassment was now taking the place of shock from earlier.

Oh. Hell.

What if she told someone? Fear prickled my skin and my chest started feeling tight. What if she told someone? What if that someone told someone and then tomorrow everyone would know that Stella Lewis, Queen Bitch, was a dyke?

I pulled out my phone and texted Kyle with shaking fingers.

Please don't tell anyone about it. Please.

I knew it sounded desperate, but I was pretty desperate. This could undo everything I'd worked for in high school. I swore I would never be the girl that everyone mocked and teased and made fun of. Just thinking about it made my stomach heave and I had to run to the bathroom. All the popcorn came back up and I gasped, resting my forehead on my arm.

Dad knocked softly.

"You okay, Star?" He had enough courtesy not to bust through the door and ask if he could hold my hair or something.

"Yeah," I said, getting to my feet and flushing the toilet. I grabbed my toothbrush and started scrubbing my teeth hard.

"Let me know if you need anything," he said before I heard him walk away from the door.

My phone buzzed and I nearly swallowed my toothbrush.

Don't worry. I won't say anything.

I slumped against the sink and spit out the toothpaste before rinsing my mouth out.

Thank you.

I left it at that. I should probably just pretend that it didn't happen. Yes. That was the best way to deal with this. Kyle wasn't going to say anything and I was sure she wanted to forget about it.

There was only one problem.

I couldn't forget about it.

———————◗◆◖———————

Late that night, in the throes of sleep, my brain took hold of the kiss and let it go further. One kiss became two and then there were tongues and hands and clothes on the floor and before I knew it I was awake and panting with my hand between my legs and the sweet burn of desire flooding my veins.

I moaned and there was no way I could get back to sleep, so I slid my hand under the waistband of my panties and got to work. I was so close that it was only a few moments later that I came, shuddering and biting my hand so I didn't moan too loudly.

Dad's room was down the hall, but I didn't want to take any chances that he'd hear me. Sometimes he stayed up late reading or doing work for his classes.

The shudders slowly stopped and I had to lay there for a second before I could even think about moving. I hadn't come that hard in a long time. And I wasn't done. The ache started up again a few seconds later and I was back at it, with the dream-kiss scenario fueling me.

Three orgasms later, I was finally done and ready to sleep. I went to the bathroom to wash my hand on semi-shaky legs.

That was when the guilt and the shame set in, but I refused to feel bad about it. I wouldn't let myself go there. I'd had plenty of fantasies about girls before, they'd just never been very specific. So I'd used Kyle to get myself off a few times, so what? It didn't mean anything. She was just there and she was cute and I'd kissed her.

Didn't.

Mean.

Anything.

Kyle

I sat in my car for a few minutes after I'd rushed out of Stella's house. Because what the fuck.

She . . . she definitely kissed me. There was no way around that. I mean, it wasn't like she'd leaned in to pluck an eyelash off my cheek, or was checking me for cavities or something. Nope. That was definitely meant to be a kiss.

It . . . kind of was, before I realized what was happening and flipped out. Because why wouldn't I flip out? Stella was . . . the last person I thought would ever kiss me. I mean, the fact that we had been yelling at each other and the next second she thought "hey, I should kiss this girl right now" was fucking crazy.

Fucking crazy.

My hands shook on the steering wheel as I gripped it. I needed something to ground me or else I was going to float away in a haze of confusion.

I should probably go. Like, right now. Definitely before her dad came home and caught me loitering in the driveway. I wouldn't even know how to explain that.

Telling myself to get my shit together, I rolled my shoulders and turned my car on. I wasn't going home right away, I couldn't. My parents would know that something had happened and then I'd have to come up with some sort of story that they'd buy. I mean, I was still going to have to do that because my parents were my parents, but at least if I had some time, I could hopefully calm myself down and come up with something good.

Nearly an hour of driving later and I didn't feel any more calm. Stella had texted me and begged me not to say anything. That hadn't even occurred to me. What kind of person did she think I was? The desperation seethed through the texts. I could almost smell it. Belatedly, it hit me that if I wanted to destroy Stella, I had the perfect ammunition.

Lucky for Stella, this wasn't a stupid, vapid teen television show where one rumor would destroy a reputation forever and a day. I didn't hate Stella. Well, maybe a little, but only because of the way she made me feel. Sure, her personality sucked sometimes, but she had her moments. They were few and far between, but they were there. We'd sort of flirted and traded barbs back and forth and I saw what she might be if she let her guard down. Also made me curious why she kept a guard up. If she wasn't a bitch, then why did she want people to think that?

Stella Lewis was a fucking mystery and I just kept sinking deeper and deeper.

I couldn't sleep that night. I was still thinking about the sort-of kiss. Trying to remember what it had felt like, but it had been too short to really judge. I'd never kissed a girl before. I mean, I'd never wanted to.

Did I want to kiss Stella?

Well, if I asked my body, then it was a resounding YES. If I asked my brain . . . it was NO followed by a very quiet yes. Followed by a no. And then another yes.

Yeah, okay, I was confused. Even more confused than before the not-kiss.

I kept trying to get comfortable and couldn't. Every position I tried I'd get uncomfortable after about five minutes. I tried everything. I pillow under my knees, my feet by the headboard, on my back, on both sides, nothing.

My mind was too busy thinking about too many things to let my body slow down long enough to get into sleep mode. I finally gave up and grabbed my phone. At least if I couldn't sleep, I had something to distract me.

I hit Tumblr and then Snapchat and, for some reason, I clicked on my Messages. The last one I'd sent or received was Stella's. Before I could tell myself that it was a bad idea, I sent her a text.

I'm not going to tell anyone. I promise. Just wanted you to know. Again.

It was totally stupid and I didn't know what she was going to think, but I went ahead and sent it anyway. Her phone was probably off, or on silent, so I didn't expect a response.

And then the little typing bubble popped up that told me she was responding. It went away and then popped up again. And went away. Popped up. Went away.

Just hit send. I can see you trying to figure out what to say.

What the hell was I doing? Ugh. I needed to stop this ASAP.

Don't tell me what to do.

I snorted, because I totally read the text in her voice.

Then don't be indecisive. Why are you even awake right now?

Her responses came quicker.

Why are you?

Texting with her is just like talking to her. Only easier because I don't get distracted by her face and her voice.

No reason.

I could just picture her face. Perfect eyebrow arched.

Uh huh. I believe you.

The sarcasm was thick with this one.

Well, I could call you a pot or a kettle so . . .

I had a stupid grin on my face and I kinda hated it, but couldn't stop it.

Oh, you're so funny. I never could have come up with that one.

I heard a sound and realized I was laughing.

You know you laughed.

Did not.

Are we arguing again? Because earlier when we did that, you decided to kiss me.

She typed for a long time after I said that.

It wasn't a kiss. Not really.

I snorted again.

Then what would you call it? Mouth-to-mouth? Because I definitely wasn't drowning.

I could hear her sighing from here.

Shut up Kyle.

You're the one answering me.

She answered with a middle finger emoji.

Cute.

There was another long pause.

I'm turning my phone off now.

I laughed to myself.

Ok. Go ahead.

I am.

Fine.

Fine.

She stopped answering after that. But I kept checking my phone into the wee hours of the morning. Just in case.

———————◆———————

I got to English early the next day and was waiting and waiting for Stella to show up. She rushed in, at the last minute and for the first time, probably in her life, she looked flustered. Her hair was messy; not in its characteristic spirals. Her face was free of makeup and she had jeans and a simple t-shirt on. She sat down without looking at me, but I couldn't stop looking at her.

Okay, so I'd pulled back when she tried to kiss me last night, but if she did it now? Looking like that?

I definitely wouldn't have pulled away. Oh no. I would have twisted my fingers in that shirt and pulled her closer so I could feel her body against mine and OH MY GOD I NEED TO STOP LOOKING AT HER RIGHT NOW.

With a herculean effort, I tore my eyes away from Stella, who hadn't moved her eyes from her notebook or acknowledged my presence.

Class. I was in class. We were learning . . . things. Our teacher was saying words.

But the blood that was supposed to be running my brain was going to other places and I kept crossing and uncrossing my legs. I had never been this fucking turned on during school hours. Was this how guys felt? Like, things were almost getting painful.

I was actually considering running out to my car to get some relief, but then something poked me in the arm. It came from my right, and there was only one person sitting on my right.

"You look like you're in pain," she hissed. It was hard for us to talk to each other without getting caught since we were in the front row, but Mr. Hurley was standing by the window on the other side of the room, waxing on about literary theory or some such bullshit. He was all caught up in it and a quick glance around the room confirmed that just about everyone else had also checked out of this particular lesson.

"I'm. Fine," I said through clenched teeth. I so wasn't fine.

"Don't look fine," she said with a bit of a sing-song.

"I. Am," I said. She really was asking for it. I turned to glare at her, but was arrested by the sight of her makeup-free face. Freckles.

She had freckles. Just a few on her cheeks, under her eyes that looked so, so beautiful. How was it that she looked better with a totally clean face? It didn't make sense.

I realized my mouth was open a little so I closed it. The only indication that she wasn't totally fine too was her appearance and the tiniest hint of pink in her cheeks.

Guess I wasn't the only one knocked off their game today.

"I think we need to talk," I said in a low voice that only she could hear.

"Right now?" she said, a hint of irritation in her tone.

"Well maybe not right now," I tried to say, but then she raised her hand and said that she had to go to the bathroom. She tossed a meaningful look over her shoulder and I got the hint. But I couldn't say that I also had to go, because that would be way too obvious. So it was time to embarrass myself in the name of talking with Stella.

"Ow! Oh my god!" I yelled out, clutching my bad leg and effectively putting a stop to the lecture.

Mr. Hurley rushed over and knelt down. Every now and then I had nerve pain, so this had happened before. But never this dramatic. I was laying it on thick.

"Is it your leg? Do you need to be excused?" he said as everyone else stared and whispered and made suggestions and some muttered words that weren't very nice. Fuck them. I didn't care.

"Yes, I think so," I said, biting my lip and hoping he believed me. It was kind of awful to take advantage like this, but I needed to get out of this class and have things out with Stella. We hadn't gotten anything out last night via our text messages. Now she couldn't run away from me and we could figure this shit out.

"You're excused. I'll email you tonight with everything you've missed. Go see the nurse." And with that, I gathered up my things and limped (harder than normal) out of the room and then resumed my regular walk. I was headed toward the bathroom when a hand reached out and yanked me into a corner shielded by a wall of lockers. We'd be pretty safe here until the bell rang in a few minutes.

"Hey, watch it," I said, yanking my arm back. She put both palms up in surrender.

"You were the one who wanted to talk. So. Talk." She crossed her arms and I tried not to stare at her chest. Somehow it was even more on view in the tight t-shirt. I could just see the line of her bra through the fabric.

Definitely not the point. I pulled my gaze up to her face. Those freckles. *Those freckles.*

"We need to talk about it. Whatever it was. I promised not to tell anyone, but I'm going to need an explanation. Because . . . what the fuck, Stella?" That was the only thing I could come up with. "I mean, did I give you some sort of signal that I wanted to kiss you or . . ." I trailed off. Oh. God. She knew. She must know. I'd been too obvious.

I opened my mouth, but nothing came out.

"No! No," Stella said the second no more quietly. Her arms uncrossed and she twisted her fingers together and looked at the floor. I'd never seen her look so . . . vulnerable.

"I don't know why it happened. I don't know what's wrong with me." She sounded small. And scared. I knew the feeling. My stomach was flipping all over the place and I almost had the urge to hug her. Just gather her in my arms and let her rest her head on my shoulder. I wanted to do that. I really wanted to do that.

"Do you? I mean, are you . . ." I couldn't finish.

"Did I try to kiss you because I like you and I'm a big fat dyke?" I

73

flinched at her words. "Don't flatter yourself."

"Uh, okay, then what was it?" Because generally, you only kiss people because you want to kiss them. Because you want your mouth and their mouth to touch as a sign of affection. I mean, I didn't have a lot of kiss experience, and none with another girl, but I was pretty sure that was how things worked.

She tossed her hands in the air and a few wisps of hair floated around her face.

"I don't know! God."

"Jesus, I'm not interrogating you. I just want to know what was going through your head," I said, trying to use a calm tone. She looked on the verge of flipping out.

"I . . . It was just . . ." She clamped her teeth down on her bottom lip and shook her head.

"You wouldn't understand."

"What would I understand?" I asked gently. She shifted her feet; ready to bolt.

"You just wouldn't, okay?" she snapped.

"Try me." I was both curious and freaked out to hear what she had to say. Because I was pretty sure I understood exactly what she was talking about and what she'd been thinking because I had been thinking the same thing about her. There was no denying it now.

I liked Stella. I really, really liked her and if she kissed me again, I'd kiss her back. I would so kiss her back.

CHAPTER 7

Stella

I shouldn't have left the classroom, but I had to get out. She was looking at me in a way that made me want to drag her out to my car and throw her in the backseat. She was still sort of doing it, actually.

I mean, I was a total hot mess, but I guess that worked for her?

I kept telling her that she wouldn't understand why I tried to kiss her, but I wasn't getting that vibe now. I was getting a completely different vibe that made my cheeks flush and my skin too tight.

I'd already told her that I didn't want to kiss her because I was into her, which was the biggest lie ever.

I liked her a lot, but I had no idea if I could trust her. She could just as easily turn on me and I couldn't handle that. I stood there, weighing the risks as she waited. She tilted her head to the side just a little and it was so unbearably cute.

"Come on," she said, lifting her chin.

"Come on what?" I said.

"Come on," she said, backing up and heading toward the door. All of my stuff was still in English, except for my purse, which was in my locker.

"Okay," I said. This was either the best decision I was ever going to make, or the worst.

Time would tell.

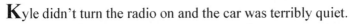

I followed Kyle out of the building, after a brief stop at my locker. We didn't say much until we were in the parking lot, presumably headed toward her car.

She stopped and unlocked the door with the press of a button on her keychain.

"Get in," she said, but it wasn't a command. It was more a question.

I looked over my shoulder toward the school. The minute I got in this car, things were going to change. They already had. They had the second I'd signed up for AP English. That first day that I looked at her and felt something new and hot swirling inside me.

I got in.

Kyle didn't turn the radio on and the car was terribly quiet.

"Where are we going?" I finally asked.

"You'll see," she said. That was it.

"If you're going to take me out to the woods and strangle me, I'd like to inform you that I've taken several self-defense classes and I think I could take you." For a moment, she took her eyes off the road and gaped at me.

Then she laughed. Such a surprised and delighted sound that it made little things in my chest start fluttering.

"You're adorable," she said when she was done, a smile lingering on her face.

"Am I?" I asked.

She sighed.

"Yes. You are. It's driving me crazy." I froze. I stopped breathing and thinking and I was pretty sure my heart stopped for a moment.

"I drive you crazy?" I asked in a small voice.

She pressed her lips together and her face flamed up. I didn't think she was going to answer.

"Just a little," she said with a wry twist of her lips. "Just a little bit, Stella." I wasn't sure what to say to that, so I didn't say anything.

Kyle kept driving and I kept stealing glances at her. Maybe more than glances. I wanted to lay in a flower-filled field and stare at her skin as shadows and sunlight played across it.

Ugh, I wanted to punch myself in the face for that thought. I was making myself sick.

I shouldn't have gotten into this car, but here I was and we were headed somewhere and . . . I had no idea what was going to happen.

I didn't like Kyle being in control. I didn't like anyone being in control of my life but me, ever.

"I don't trust you," I said.

"Oh, I'm sure you don't trust anyone. Even yourself." Ouch. She'd hit too close to home on that one.

"Shut up," I said. Brilliant response. She laughed a little.

"You don't like it when other people figure things out about you either."

"Just stop talking." I was getting more and more irritated and annoyed.

"I never should have gotten in this stupid car with you. I have no idea why I did," I said, crossing my arms.

"But you did, Stella. You did get in the car and now here we are."

Here we were.

"And also, here we are," she said, stopping the car.

We'd arrived at the lighthouse. I'd been here before on class trips and so forth, but not in the fall. In the summer the parking lot was be jammed with tourists, but now there were just a few cars here and there.

And us.

"Come on," she said again. And again, I did what she said. We both got out and I wrapped my arms around myself because it was always chillier on the coast than inland.

"Here," Kyle said, handing me a sweatshirt. I gave her a look, but she just shoved it at me. Reluctantly, I put it on. And almost passed out because it smelled like her. The sleeves were a bit too long, so I rolled them up. Kyle coughed and I turned to find her staring at me, her face red.

"It . . . it looks good on you," she said, looking at the gravel parking lot.

"Thanks," I said. "So should we . . . ?" She nodded and we walked, not toward the lighthouse, which stood like a tall white sentry protecting boats from the ravages of the rocks below, but toward those rocks.

A portion of them jutted out into the ocean, like granite fingers. Kyle and I picked our way down and headed toward the water, but not too close. One nasty fall could send you tumbling into the water, and you probably wouldn't make it out alive. The water rushed and smashed against the rocks, as if it had a vendetta against them.

I could understand that anger.

Kyle and I sat on a rock that was far enough away from the water that we wouldn't get sprayed, but close enough that we were surrounded by the rushing sound and it felt a little bit dangerous. As if we were on the edge of something dark and all-consuming that didn't care about us and our problems.

"Why did you bring me here?" I asked, pushing my hair back. It kept blowing in my face. Kyle reached into her pocket and pulled out a hair tie, handing it to me without a word. I tried to pull my hair back like hers, but I could feel that it didn't look half as good.

"Not sure. I just always come here when I need to think about something. I know it's cliché, but I don't care. Hashtag deep-thoughts." I laughed a little and she looked at me.

"This is kind of crazy, isn't it?" she asked.

"Yeah, you could say that." She scooted a little bit closer to me. Our legs were almost touching.

"Do you? I mean, you kissed me because you wanted to. And I freaked out. And I'm assuming you think it was because I didn't want you to kiss me," she said, tracing a black vein in the rock we sat on.

I couldn't move. If a wave came right then, it would sweep me away and I wouldn't move to get out of its way. The ocean churned and I waited for her to continue.

She didn't.

"Did you want me to kiss you?" My words were so soft, they were almost lost to the noise surrounding us.

Her response was even quieter, but I would have heard it in a room with a thousand other voices.

"Yes."

We stared at one another and something crackled between us. And then I was leaning forward and she was leaning forward and our mouths were meeting. We both initiated it this time and the brush of Kyle's lips over mine didn't stop. Didn't end.

It was delicate, hesitant. She shook just a little. A whisper against my mouth, but we both waited. Held onto that moment.

It was unlike any other kiss I'd ever had and I melted into her. One of my hands slipped up to cup her cheek and the other wound around the back of her neck. Her hands were on me too, but not to push me away.

To pull me closer.

Her mouth opened and her tongue darted out to tease the seam of my lips. It was sweet and a little aggressive at the same time and I moaned in the back of my throat because hell, she tasted so good. Completely different than kissing anyone else.

Our tongues touched so carefully and then something ignited and we were devouring one another. Her nails dug into my skin and the little jolt of pain made it even better. She stole my breath and my lungs ached, but I couldn't stop.

Kyle could. She pulled away and I opened my eyes to see hers. Behind her glasses, her eyes were green. So green.

Beautiful.

"Wow," she breathed over my lips and I almost reached out to capture her mouth again.

I couldn't talk.

"So that's what it's like to kiss a girl," she said, moving her face away and studying me. Her lips were a little red and her cheeks were flushed.

I could stare at her forever.

"Stella, can you say something? I really need to know what you're thinking right now." I opened my mouth and then licked my lips. They tasted like her. I shuddered and gathered myself.

"I don't know what I'm thinking, Kyle. I have no idea. All I can think about is that I want to kiss you again."

"Really?" Her face broke into the sweetest smile ever.

"Yes. Really." She let out a breath, as if she was relieved.

"Fuck, I was scared there for a minute, thinking I was the only one. Because holy fuck, Stella." I wanted to roll my eyes at the excessive cursing, but I couldn't.

"I know. I know." That was all I could say.

"So we should probably do it again. Like right now, yes?"

"Yes."

Who knew that Stella Lewis was an amazing kisser? I mean, seriously. Like a stop your heart, make you feel like you're going to die, never want it to end kind of kiss. The kiss to end all kisses.

Kiss wasn't even the right word. That was so much more than just a kiss. We should invent a new word for that. Maybe after we stopped kissing each other we could. I mean, if we stopped. I didn't want to and the way she was moaning and making these cute little noises, I could get the idea that she didn't either.

My ass was completely numb on the rock, but I couldn't have cared less. All I wanted was to keep my lips attached to hers as long as possible.

I tried to take my glasses off because they were getting in the way, but she told me to leave them on.

Unfortunately, we had to stop, but only because her phone buzzed with a text.

She jumped away from me and fumbled for her phone. I sat there and waited as she frowned and typed out a response to the message. As I freaked the fuck out. I'd just made out with a girl. I'D JUST MADE OUT WITH A GIRL.

"Just Midori. Asking where I was."

"Oh, right," I said, still dazed by the kissing. I could feel the echo of her hands on the back of my neck.

"So . . ." I said, dragging the word out. "That happened."

"Yeah, it did," she said, as she took a strand of her hair and wound it around her fingers.

"And it was good. Really good."

"Yes."

"And now we have to figure out what the fuck to do from here."

She nodded slowly and stared out at the waves. Deep blue, topped with whitecaps here and there.

"I don't know what this means. I don't know if this means that I like you, which is crazy to begin with because you're kind of awful, or if I like . . . girls, or if I like boys and girls, and I'm really, really confused." The words tumbled out of my mouth, tripping over one another.

Stella listened and twirled her hair.

"You think I'm an awful person?" she asked.

"I didn't mean it that way, but kind of?" How was it that I could want her so much, but also know that she wasn't the nicest of people? How could I be so attracted to her and completely ignore that?

"No, you're right. I am an awful person. I like it that way." She turned back toward me, her mouth a thin line.

"Why?" I just didn't get it.

Her eyes narrowed.

"Because. You wouldn't understand." It was like she'd slammed a wall between us and I felt the chill of the ocean air at last. I wrapped my arms around myself.

"You're going to shut me out. Just like that?" She raised her chin.

"Just like that."

Unbelievable.

"Okay, fine, fuck you, too." I slid away from her on the rock and contemplated stomping back to the car like a petulant child.

"Look, don't act like just because you had your tongue down my throat that you know me now. You don't."

"Yeah, well, I know that you don't have to be a bitch all the fucking time. Not to me." My stupid voice cracked on the last word.

"You're pretty presumptuous, you know that? What do you think's going to happen? That we're going to kiss some more and then hold hands in the hallway and go to prom and get crowned queen and queen? This is the real world and stuff like that doesn't just happen." Her words were sharp and sliced across my skin.

"Well obviously I know that's not going to happen, Stella, I'm not a fucking idiot. But there's something here and I think we need to at least . . . I don't know, give it a chance." I tossed my hands in the air. I didn't even know what I was saying.

She pushed herself off from the rock and started picking her way back to the car. Joke was on her, since I had the keys.

"You can't just walk away from this," I called after her.

"Watch me," she yelled back.

Oh, I was. She was in excellent shape from cheerleading. Amazing legs.

I had no control over the fact that I was definitely into her. In that I wanted her naked with my hands all over her.

Two hours ago, that thought would have freaked me the fuck out, but now it was just . . . there. It was there and it didn't feel wrong. I didn't get this twisting in the pit of my stomach telling me to stop thinking things like that. No.

It felt right. Easy. So. Damn. Easy. How had I not figured this out by now? I didn't need Google. I only needed the way she kissed and the way she felt and the way I wanted her.

Fuck, did I want her.

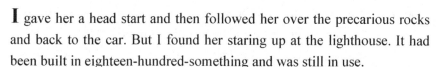

I gave her a head start and then followed her over the precarious rocks and back to the car. But I found her staring up at the lighthouse. It had been built in eighteen-hundred-something and was still in use.

"Whatcha looking at?" I asked and she startled a little at the sound of my voice. There was only one other car in the parking lot now, way down the end of the lot.

"Nothing," she muttered. She'd tucked her hands inside the sleeves of my sweatshirt and her anger seemed to have cooled off again.

"Do you want to go back on the rocks and make out?" I asked, only half-joking.

"No."

"Okayyyyy. Wanna make out in my car?" She fixed me with a withering look.

"No. I don't want to make out with you." I snorted out a laugh.

"Yeah, okay. Sure."

Stella turned her back on me and then . . . her shoulders started shaking. Either she was laughing or crying. Pretty sure it was the latter.

"Hey," I said, putting my hand on her shoulder. She tried to throw me off, but didn't resist when I turned her back around.

Yup. Crying.

"Hey, what's the matter?" I mean, I could probably guess, but I wanted to hear it from her.

She just shook her head and then just kind of fell into my arms. At first I didn't know what to do but after a second of being stunned, I wrapped my arms around her and she buried her head on my shoulder as she kept crying.

"It's okay. It's gonna be okay," I said, because what else was I supposed to say? I wasn't really good at this kind of thing. Grace was much better. She always had the right words at the right time.

My hands ran up and down her back in what I hoped was a soothing way. No idea if I was helping or not, but she was just sniffling now.

Stella raised her head and wiped her eyes. She looked ridiculously good for someone who had been crying. Using the sleeve of my sweatshirt, she swiped her nose and eyes. I didn't mind at all.

I kept my hands on her shoulders.

"Stella. Talk to me. Please talk to me. I know you think that I don't know you, but I know a few things." She huffed and rolled her eyes, as if this was one giant inconvenience when she'd been the one crying two seconds ago.

"It's nothing. I just . . . I had a plan, you know? I was going to get through high school and then when I got to college, I'd go full gay and meet a girl and I'd finally be able to be myself. But then you had to come and . . ." she trailed off and put one of her hands on my chest, just below my throat.

"Everything was working fine until I signed up for AP English and sat next to you and started to feel things that I didn't want to feel. I was going to ignore it but then we got paired up and I couldn't anymore." She sniffed again.

"Yeah, I know the feeling. Except I was totally going to date guys when I got to college. So this is a little weird for me." That was an understatement.

"You didn't know? That you liked girls?" I shook my head. It was hard to think with her hand there, her fingers just barely sneaking under the collar of my shirt to caress my skin.

"Oh. I figured you did. That was probably why you freaked out so much when I kissed you, huh?" She laughed once.

"Yeah, maybe that was it," I said, my tone dripping with sarcasm. But then I looked at her face and realized I was being harsh. "Fuck, Stella. I had no idea."

"Yeah, well. No one does. Until you." Until me. Stella Lewis liked girls. And had for a while. Thoughts and questions were popping in my brain and I was getting close to overload.

"I think I need to like, sit down for a minute," I said, and this time she took my hand and led me to the car.

———————◗◆◖———————

"So have you ever been attracted to guys?" I asked after I'd sat with everything for a few minutes.

"I don't think so. I mean, I've dated and kissed them, but it's not what I would choose. So no, I'm not bisexual. If that was what you were asking," she said. Clearly, she was a lot more comfortable with . . .

everything than I was.

"Oh, wow, there are so many things going through my head right now," I said, resting my head on the steering wheel.

"So I'm guessing this is all new for you?" she asked softly.

I nodded against the wheel and then raised my head.

"I mean, yeah. I just . . . I have no idea when it started, but it turned into a thing and now I don't even know what to do or what to think. I tried Googling it, but couldn't follow through." There was a cute little snort next to me.

"You Googled it?" She gave me a look as if she thought that was precious.

"Yeah. What did you do?" Why was that outrageous? Google had never failed me before.

She pulled her hair out of the elastic and it tumbled over her shoulders. The fact that I was just this year learning I was attracted to her seemed ridiculous. How could I not be attracted to her?

"I don't know. I was like, thirteen? I think I just assumed everyone looked at girls that way. Because girls are beautiful and pretty and why wouldn't you want them? Took me a little while to realize that wasn't the case and I had to hide it. But I never denied it to myself. I know who I am, Kyle."

"Wow," I said. "I had no idea." She gave me a wry smile.

"It's not something I want anyone to know. At least not now. I was going to head to college and be a completely different person in a different place." She looked out the window at the ocean.

"I know what you mean," I murmured. I'd thought the same thing. "I mean, I was going to wait until college to date guys. But now I'm not sure if I want to. Date guys." My head started spinning again and my stomach growled. This had been one of the longest days ever and I was starving.

"Do you want to get something to eat?" I blurted out.

"Sure," she said.

Because we lived in a small ass town and there would have been questions if we went somewhere alone, and discussed the things we were going to discuss, we went back to my house. My parents were at work, so I didn't have to worry.

It was a fine plan until I remembered that it wasn't that clean and it was smaller than and not as nice as hers.

"Um, yeah. So . . . this is it," I said, waving my arm around and cringing inwardly. I waited as Stella's eyes swept the room and then she headed toward the kitchen. As if she'd lived here for years. I followed in her wake as she popped open the fridge and stuck her head in.

"What are you in the mood for?" I gaped at her back as she bent down and pawed through the crisper drawers.

"Um, my own food because this is my house?" I said and she straightened.

"Well, I'm in the mood for something smothered in cheese." She slammed the fridge shut and opened the freezer.

"Aha!" she said, pulling something out. "This will do."

It was a box of frozen spinach and artichoke dip.

"Do you have some chips or something . . ." she trailed off as she searched the counters and then grabbed a bag of tortilla chips.

I watched as she read the instructions on the box, set the oven to preheat, found a bowl to put the chips in and then handed me a soda.

"Um, thanks."

"Sure," she said with a little smile. I'd never seen her so . . . relaxed? No, that wasn't the right word. Un-frozen? Warm. I'd never seen her this warm.

Even the way she moved was different. More like when she was cheering.

She hopped up on the counter and munched on a chip as the dip cooked in the oven.

"Make yourself at home," I said and she pushed the bowl of chips toward me. I nudged over the little step I used in the kitchen to help me climb up onto the counter.

"So, am I the first girl you've ever had a crush on?" she asked and a chip crumb went down my windpipe and caused me to cough.

"Uh, I guess so? I'm not really sure."

"You're not. My first, I mean." She sighed, as if at a good memory. "Shannon O'Shea. I was eleven and she was fourteen. God, she was so beautiful. I used to imagine just running up and kissing her on the cheek, and spent hours fantasizing about holding her hand. Then she got a boyfriend and went to high school. You never forget your first, though."

I gaped at her.

"Are you drunk right now?" There was no way, but holy shit, she was telling me all kinds of things without me even prodding her.

"Haha, no. I'm just . . . I haven't had anyone to talk to about this so it's all kind of coming out at once. Sorry." She shrugged one shoulder and grabbed another chip, smiling as she bit into it.

"Yeah, me neither. But I didn't think I was ready? I don't know. I'm still . . ." I trailed off.

"Hey," she said, brushing a hand down my shoulder. It made me shiver inside. Just being near her was driving me crazy. I wanted to dramatically swipe the bowl of chips off the counter and tackle her and do a lot of other things that involved tongues and fingers and secret places.

The timer dinged and I nearly fell off the counter, but I needed to put some space between me and Stella.

I nearly reached for the little tub of hot dip without an oven mitt, but at the last second I remembered.

"It's probably still too hot, so," I said, fumbling as I set the dip on top of another oven mitt. "Um, do you want to maybe sit in the living room?"

I really had no idea how to handle this situation. I was flying without a safety net and I was freaking out. Stella seemed so comfortable and I wished I could be like her.

"Sure," she said, pushing herself off the counter and grabbing the bowl of chips. "Lead the way."

CHAPTER 8

Stella

It was adorable how nervous she was. It was almost like a movie, how our hands collided as we both reached for a chip at the same time. Kyle blushed and yanked her hand back. So far, we'd been sitting in her living room eating steadily through the chips and dip and not talking.

I was fine with silence, but she was fidgeting and it was super distracting. Seeing Kyle flustered was fun.

"Do your parents know?" I asked and she froze. Her face went white. Okay, guess that hadn't been the right question to ask. I wasn't one to talk. I hadn't told Dad or Gabe and had no intention of it for a long time.

"Uh, no. *I* didn't even know. I still don't really know. I think I need to figure things out before I tell them anything." We were down to just chip crumbs in the bowl and I kept picking the smaller ones, leaving the bigger ones for her.

"That's probably smart. You might wake up tomorrow and totally be straight." I grinned at her and she gaped at me in surprise before smacking me on the shoulder.

"Brat."

I shrugged.

"I'm just saying. I know this one time I hit my head a little too hard at practice and that night I dreamed about dicks. So many dicks. I was just surrounded by them. Mmmmm . . ." That really shocked her. But that was my goal.

She burst out laughing and it was totally worth it. Her face lit up and it was a whole other level of cute for her.

I was in serious trouble.

We lounged on the couch and flipped through the channels.

"There are never enough shows with lesbians," I said.

"Aren't there any? I never really noticed." Oh, sweet gayby. I kept forgetting that she was so new to this. But maybe I could educate her. That would be fun. Potentially in a lot of ways.

"You're different," she said after a few minutes of silence. She wasn't looking at me and had taken off her glasses to polish them on the hem of her t-shirt.

"What do you mean?" I asked, but I knew exactly what she meant. I wasn't being a heinous bitch was what she meant.

"Well, you're not . . . um . . ." She pushed her glasses up on her nose and waved her hands as if she was looking for the right word.

"A bitch?" I finished. Her face went a little red.

"I wouldn't necessarily put it that way." I rolled my eyes.

"Yeah, you would. You and everyone else. I know what people say about me, Kyle. It doesn't bother me." Not even a little. It was so much better than the alternative.

"It doesn't?" I shook my head. I expected that to be the end of the questioning, but it wasn't.

"Why not?"

"Because I don't care what they think." This was a lie, but she didn't need to know. I wasn't sure what this thing was between us, but it definitely wasn't going anywhere. We weren't going to hold hands and ride off into the gay sunset.

"Really?" She raised one eyebrow, calling my bluff. I gave her the same look.

"Really."

She went to say something else, but then all the blood drained from her face.

"What time is it?"

"Um, four thirty," I said, checking my phone that I'd set on the coffee table.

"Crap, my mom is going to be home any minute. I hate to do this to you, but you've got to go. My parents are insane and if you want to not be interrogated about every single detail of your life, I would leave now." I knew her parents were a little obsessive and I definitely didn't want to have a conversation with a mom about who I was and what I was doing here.

"Point taken," I said, getting off the couch, grabbing the empty chip bowl and the disposable dip bowl and heading back to the kitchen.

"You didn't have to do that," Kyle said, trailing after me. I just shrugged again and turned to face her.

"Well. I guess I'll see you in class." It was an anticlimactic end to what had been a strange day.

"Yeah, see you in class." I almost leaned in to kiss her, but she just stared at me in that cute-but-stunned way and I couldn't do it.

"Okay then." I pivoted on my heels and headed out the front door.

That was when I realized she'd been the one to drive us here.

****

I stood outside for a minute, wondering what to do, but there was no option but to go back inside, which was what I was preparing to do when the front door opened and she walked out.

"Oh, yeah. I forgot that you didn't have your car here. I can drive you back." I nodded and got in the passenger seat.

"I had fun today," I said and then cringed. I sounded like an idiot.

"Me too," Kyle said, turning the car on.

She drove in silence for a few minutes, her hands clamped on the steering wheel.

"So, what happens now?" Kyle said.

"What do you mean?" Once again, I knew exactly what she meant.

"I mean, with you and me. Not that there is a you and me. I don't even know what the hell happened today other than we made out and I would really, really like to do it again." Fuck, that made me want to tell her to pull over so I could yank her into the backseat.

"Are you saying that you want to come out, and then be my girlfriend?" I asked, not looking at her.

"Oh, no. We can't do that." No, we couldn't.

"So there are two options. One, pretend this never happened and go back to hating each other, or two, we make out when no one else is around." I hoped she would go for the second option, because it involved more kissing. I was in favor of any plan where I could kiss Kyle some more. That girl knew what she was doing and would have been totally wasted on boys.

"So, be like secret girlfriends?" I wanted to roll my eyes at that. It sounded stupid. Like a plot of a bad movie.

"No. We'd just be two girls who sometimes hang out and kiss. And potentially do other things. No pressure. But I don't think we should like, be best friends or something." I already had one of those and I didn't need another one. Besides, I didn't want to be Kyle's friend. I wanted to kiss her until she couldn't breathe. That wasn't usually a friendship activity. Unless you were friends with benefits, but that wasn't for me either.

"Okay, but what would we call it?" I sighed.

"Why do we have to call it anything?" I asked, turning to her. We were almost to the school.

"I guess we don't have to." No, we didn't. We didn't owe anyone anything.

"So how will this work?" She asked so many damn questions. I was going to have to kiss her more so she'd stop.

"No idea. We'll figure it out. Just text or call or whatever. And don't act any different at school. Promise." That was very important. I didn't want anyone catching on that things had changed between me and Kyle.

"Uh huh." She still looked a little dazed. I had the feeling she was going to be up late tonight. So would I, but for different reasons. I was going to spend a lot of time thinking about kissing her and what that tongue of hers could do if it were applied to places other than my mouth.

She pulled into the parking lot and I realized that if I didn't hurry, I was going to be late for cheer practice.

"I have to go. So I'll see you around," I said, my hand on the door.

"Yeah, okay," she said, giving me a little jerky nod. I got out and closed the door, thanking the stars that there was no one around to see me get out of Kyle's car.

What a bizarre day. I couldn't stop thinking about how things had changed in only a few hours. Just last night Stella had kissed me and today I was making out with her and now I was gay.

I mean, I'd sort of known? But kissing Stella and wanting her kind of cemented it. My parents were mad at dinner when I wasn't as open about my day as I could have been so I escaped to my room and shut the door.

I just wanted some time to THINK. There was so much noise in my head and I couldn't sort out any of it.

Yes, I liked Stella. But was it just her or other girls?

I knew the answer to that. Yes, it was other girls. No one specific (until now), just . . . girls. Their hair and the way they walked and not to mention the way their bodies were. Just perfectly shaped. It was everything about them. How had I been so blind to it?

That was what got me. How could I live eighteen years and not know? If I hadn't known this about myself, what else didn't I know? That was the scariest part.

And my parents. What would they say? What would they think? They'd struggled and pushed me to be the absolute best and to have a better life than they'd had. How would me being gay change that? Sure, marriage was legal all over the United States, but that wasn't everything. There was so much more.

They weren't anti-gay, but I didn't know how they would feel about having a gay daughter. If I was gay. I guess technically I was a lesbian? How did I decide what I wanted to be called?

There were just so many questions that I didn't have answers to. So I asked someone who might.

Do I have to call myself a lesbian now?

I knew she would be up.

No. You can be gay or queer or whatever you want. You don't owe anyone a label.

She sounded so different now. It just blew my mind how I had known her for so many years and not know what she was really like. It was obvious to me now that she put on a bitchy front, but I didn't know why. Her real personality was great. She was snarky and funny and thoughtful. At least she'd been that way today. Why would she hide that? I didn't get it.

Are you still going to be a raging bitch to me in English?

I felt like I could hear her laughing.

Absolutely. What you saw today was an anomaly.

But WHY?

I knew I wasn't going to get a straight answer from her so I changed the topic.

Do you know anyone else who's gay?

I could think of a few kids off the top of my head and I knew there was some sort of rainbow organization. I'd never really paid attention to it because I didn't think it was for me. Guess I was wrong.

Yeah, there's a group of them.

Was I now required to be friends with them? I had so many questions about this. There really should be a rulebook.

You don't have to do anything you don't want to, Kyle. Seriously.

I knew that, but I almost wished there was someone standing next to me and telling me what the rules were, what the steps were. I had so much uncertainty. Part of me even wondered if I'd just made a huge mistake or had a brain tumor or something.

I know. I guess I just have to get used to it.

She took a long while to respond and I saw her typing and then deleting a few messages before she sent one.

I'm here if you need me.

The words hit me like a punch. How had this Stella existed and I had no idea?

Thanks. We should probably go to bed. School night and everything.

This time her response was lightning fast.

We could always pass the time by sexting. What are you wearing?

For a half-second I thought she was serious and I realized just how much I would enjoy that. And then she sent a little winky face and I wanted to kick myself for thinking that. Of course she was joking. We had literally just kissed today. I mean, last night too, but it had been only about 24 hours from the first lip contact. Sexting was getting a little ahead of things.

Wouldn't you like to know . . .

I hoped she was laughing.

Yeah. I would.

Wait, was she serious? This had been the most confusing day ever. Thank God tomorrow was Thursday and I wouldn't see her in class.

But that meant that I'd see her on Friday and then at the game. Stella was definitely going to be there and I had no idea how I was going to handle that situation. Some of my other friends might not notice, but Grace definitely would know something was up with me. That was what best friends were for.

I realized I hadn't responded to Stella in a while.

I sleep naked I typed and hit Send before I could second-guess myself.

So do I.

Well, shit. This was definitely not helping. I was turned on as fuck and I only had myself to blame. I shouldn't have texted her.

Goodnight, babe.

I groaned into my pillow. What was she *doing* to me?

CHAPTER 9

Stella

I was still thinking about the text messages and the kisses and everything about Kyle when I woke up the next morning. My blood still felt like it was on fire and didn't want to cool anytime soon.

Kyle Blake was going to be the death of me. Fortunately I only caught a glance or two of her in the hallways on Thursday. If I saw her every day I didn't know how I'd handle that. It was too much already.

Thursday I had a shift at the vet clinic and I was totally out of it. I messed up several times and my boss actually asked me if I was okay and suggested that maybe I should go home early. I wanted to kick myself for getting so distracted by the hot nerd.

She didn't text or reach out to me at all that day, so our first contact was on Friday in class. She got there first and I slid into my seat beside her. At least she didn't flinch.

"Hey," I said and she looked at me as if I'd done something completely insane.

"What?" I said, looking around, but no one was paying attention to us. They were all on their phones or talking to each other.

Kyle leaned closer and I told myself not to inhale too deeply and remember how her mouth tasted.

Tried and failed on both counts.

"I thought we were going back to the status quo. You never said 'hey' to me before," she said in a low voice, eyes darting around as if we were going to get busted for just talking to one another.

I rolled my eyes.

"We can at least be cordial without raising too much suspicion," I said. At the beginning, I hadn't wanted to set off any potential red flags, but the more I tried to avoid Kyle, the more obvious it was that I was trying to avoid her. So maybe if I allowed myself a little contact, things would be okay.

A cynical voice in the back of my mind told me that it was a stupid plan and that someone was going to catch on, but I told the voice to shut the fuck up. That same voice would be telling me to go for it if it had had the chance to make out with Kyle.

"Oh, we can?" she asked, raising one eyebrow. I wanted to grab her face and kiss the shit out of her, but that would definitely not be a good idea at this moment.

"Yes, we can," I breathed, leaning a little closer and smiling in satisfaction as she swallowed hard.

Mr. Hurley started class then and our heads snapped forward at the same time. Not suspicious at all.

"My dad looked over our paper on Thursday night," I said when Mr. Hurley told us to keep working together in groups as he wandered around the room and "kept us on task." There were only a few groups that needed him to hover to make sure they were doing work and not screwing off. Kyle and I were not one of them, so he generally left us to our own devices.

"And?" Kyle said, looking at the printout I'd given her with my dad's correction marks on it. There weren't many.

"And he said it was good. So I think we're pretty much set." She flipped through the pages, her eyes scanning before she set it back on her desk and turned to me.

"So, what now? We're basically done and we have a whole week to work on this." I wasn't sure, so I raised my hand and Mr. Hurley came over. I told him the situation and he just gave me a smile.

"I had the feeling you were going to be an overachiever in this class, Stella. Are you sure you're absolutely finished with everything?" We nodded in unison. He sighed.

"You have two options. You can either use the next few classes as time to work on an extra credit project, or I can send you to the library to work on something else." I glanced at Kyle. I knew what option I wanted.

"Library, I think," Kyle said and I nodded. Good. That had been my choice. The library was full of all kinds of corners and nooks and there were rarely people up there during the school day, so we would potentially have privacy.

Mr. Hurley wrote us both notes and we hurried as fast as we could out the door.

"I can't believe he let us do that," Kyle said as I slowed my pace to match hers.

"He knows my dad so I think he lets me get away with a lot," I said with a smirk. Kyle rolled her eyes as we headed out of the English building and toward the library. It was at the top floor, so we got to take the special elevator.

"Look at you with your fancy key," I said when Kyle pulled it out of her back pocket and put it in the hole above the buttons to unlock it.

"If I had to take the stairs, I would get there about the time class was over." Ninety percent of the time I didn't even think about her limp, but then we'd be confronted by something like stairs and I'd remember that it wasn't as easy for her to get around as it was for me.

"No way," Kyle said as we strolled into the library and looked around. There was no one in sight. Not even the librarian. But then she bustled around the corner with a stack of books in her arms and glared at us as if we'd walked into her house without permission.

"We have notes," I said, extending my hand out. She snatched them and looked at them as if they were fake IDs or something. After deciding on their authenticity, she told us to find a corner and be quiet and that if we caused any shenanigans, we would be booted out.

"No problem," I said, jerking my head in the direction of one of the corners. Kyle nodded and followed me. It was in a little alcove and had two beanbag chairs crammed in between the stacks. The only way you could see us if you walked between those exact rows of shelves and looked around part of the wall. It was perfect and almost private.

I set my stuff down and held out my hand to Kyle. She blushed but then accepted it as I helped her flop onto one of the beanbags as I crashed on the other.

"This is perfect," she said in a whisper.

"I think we can talk at almost normal volume, but I've never tested that theory," I said, a little louder than a whisper.

"Do you come here a lot?" she asked as she pulled a bag of gummy bears out of her backpack and offered me some. I took a handful as she did the same. Food was forbidden in the library, but we'd only get caught if the librarian happened to check on us and we'd have advance warning from her footsteps. So we were good.

"Not a lot, but I love libraries. Wherever I go, I always have to visit the library." I didn't know why I was telling her that. It was something only Gabe and Dad knew about. My desire to visit hundreds of libraries in hundreds of countries someday.

Kyle snorted and I pelted her with a gummy bear.

"Hey, don't waste those." She picked it up off the floor and made a face at it, but then put it in her mouth.

"Ew! Do you know what kind of germs there could be on that?" She just grinned and kept chewing.

"You just don't seem like a library kind of girl. I mean, no offense." I narrowed my eyes.

"Why? Because I'm a cheerleader? We're all supposed to be bitchy airheads, right?" She crumpled the empty bag and shoved it in her backpack.

"You know that's not what I mean. It doesn't matter that you are a cheerleader. You just seem more the social butterfly type than the library type."

"Why can't I be both?" She opened her mouth to respond, but then nodded.

"I guess you're right." I twirled a curl around my finger.

"People aren't just one thing, Kyle." She nodded.

"You mean like people aren't just lesbians?" I hadn't been talking about that, but sure. That was a good example.

"Exactly." She nodded again.

"And you're not just a hot nerd," I said, bumping my shoulder with hers.

I was rewarded by a blush that made me want to grab her face and lick her cheeks. I really had self-control issues around this girl.

"You think I'm hot?" she asked, looking down at her feet as she set her chin on her pulled-up knees.

"Kyle. Have you *seen* you?" She gaped at me.

"Um, yeah, I see myself in the mirror and it's nothing to lose your shit over, I'm pretty sure. And no one's going to put me on a magazine anytime soon."

"That's just because people are fucking idiots. You're gorgeous. Like, it's really hard for me to *not* look at you." She started to laugh.

"Are you serious?" I nodded.

"Yeah, it's a real problem. You've got that sexy nerd thing and I'm pretty sure it's designed to drive me crazy." She bit her lip to hide a smile.

"No one's ever called me sexy before." A year ago, I probably wouldn't have. But now it was so obvious to me that I couldn't ignore it even if I wanted to. She took her hair down and started to put it up again.

"Wait," I said.

She froze, her hands pulling her hair back from her face to pile it on top of her head again.

"What?"

"Let your hair down," I said, hating how breathless my voice sounded. But I'd pictured Kyle with her hair tumbling over her shoulders so many times and I just wanted to see it for real.

She gave me a look but let her hair drop, settling on her shoulders like a mahogany cape.

"It's gorgeous," I said, reaching out and running a few strands through my fingers. She didn't flinch, or tell me to stop.

"I always think I want to cut it because it drives me crazy, but I don't know if I could rock short hair." She could rock anything and look gorgeous.

I let go of her hair.

"But then your hair always looks perfect, Stella." I scoffed. My hair definitely didn't always look perfect and I spent a fair amount of time on it every day anyway.

"*You* always look perfect," Kyle said in a lower voice and now I was the one blushing.

"Thanks," I said, biting my lip. We both laughed a little.

"This is a little awkward, isn't it?" Kyle said and I nodded. Neither of us really knew how to do this. If Kyle was a boy, it would be different. So different.

Girls were complicated. Me being one didn't make Kyle any easier to figure out.

"Do you want to do something this weekend?" I blurted out. I knew that I couldn't go the whole weekend without seeing her, that was for sure.

"Um, sure. What did you have in mind?" Making out with you and maybe convincing you to take off your clothes? But I didn't say that.

"There's not a whole lot to do. Maybe we could go shopping or drive around or something." I didn't care as long as it involved her mouth and my mouth.

"Well, uh, my parents are going to this thing on Saturday to learn about financial aid for college and won't be home until late." Perfect. "You could come over. If you want." Yes. I did want.

"Sounds good. Do you want me to bring a pizza or something?"

My heart fluttered at the idea of an entire day with Kyle when we didn't have to worry about being caught.

"Yeah, that'd be great." Silence descended on us again.

"Are you going to come to the game tonight?" I'd gotten used to seeing her in the first row of bleachers. Most of the time I cheered directly to her, as if the other fans didn't even exist. I didn't mean to do it; it just happened. I had Kyle blinders.

"Yeah, do you not want me to? Would it be weird?" I put my hand on her arm.

"No. No, it wouldn't be weird. I want you there. I like it when you watch me." It sounded more intimate than I meant it and Kyle blushed again and ducked to hide a smile.

"It doesn't hurt that you look hot as fuck in your uniform." I raised one eyebrow.

"Is that so?" She sighed and tilted her head back, looking at me out of the corner of her eyes.

"You *know* you do, babe." It was hot as fuck when she called me "babe." I'd always found guys giving their girlfriends cutesy nicknames to be patronizing, but I think I was finally understanding it. It made my insides feel like warm mush and my skin all prickly. In a good way. A very good way.

"Oh, well. Sorry?" She shoved my shoulder and I tipped back so she fell against me.

"Sorry!" she said, trying to scramble off me, but I clamped my hands on her arms.

"Don't be." I couldn't take it anymore and I pushed myself up so I could kiss her. Just a little one. Just because it had been so long. Like, more than twenty-four hours, which was basically an eternity.

Kyle let out a tiny little moan and I had to stop myself from pulling her on top of me so I could feel her body pressing against mine.

But she pulled away, looking over her shoulder, as if she was going to find the librarian standing above us and glaring down in disapproval.

Of course no one was there.

"We shouldn't," she said, sitting up again. I sighed. She was probably right. I didn't know how the administration would deal with finding two girls making out in the library. Probably not as well as they would if one of us was a boy. Fucked up, but true.

And this was exactly why I'd wanted to wait until college for all this. And then Kyle Blake came and smashed all my plans.

"It's okay," I said, reaching out to stroke one finger down her cheek so she knew I wasn't mad. "We should be careful. You're right. I guess you're the one with the most common sense out of the both of us." I laughed a little under my breath and then the bell rang, making is both jump.

"We should go," I said as I stood up and held a hand out to Kyle. She took it and didn't let go right away. I had a brief flash of what it could be like, if she didn't let go and we walked out of here together, still holding hands. What would happen? Would people stare and scream at us for being dykes? Or would they not even notice? Or would they spit on us? There was just no way to know for sure. And then we'd have to tell our parents and hell to the no.

Kyle gave me a sad little smile, as if she was sorry before she dropped her hand.

"We should probably leave separately," she said and I nodded.

"I'll go first, I guess." She shrugged one shoulder. I started to walk away. Another anti-climactic ending for us. We seemed to have a lot of them.

"I'll text you later," she said with a wink and I couldn't keep the smile off my face.

"Later," I said, giving her a little wave as I walked away with a bounce in my step.

I couldn't believe I'd asked her to come over. Again. But I wanted to see her and that was the best option. I didn't want to take the chance that if we went out that we'd see someone from school or someone's parent or someone else from this damn small town. Gossip spread quicker than a wildfire in a field of dry grass. Everyone knew everyone's business, no matter how small or insignificant.

Fortunately, Stella got it, which made things a lot easier. If I could use that word in this situation, which wasn't very easy at all.

I was still coming to terms with the fact that I liked her and wanted her. Why now? Why *her*?

"Your face is all red, are you okay?" Grace asked as we headed down to the field for the football game. Of course most of the town was here, because what else was there to do on a Friday night in Maine? Other than drive out to someone's gravel pit and get drunk and shoot shit with a pellet gun, which was probably what the people who weren't here were currently doing.

"Yeah, fine, why?" I'd been blowing Grace off a bit, claiming that I was stressed with schoolwork, but that wasn't going to fly. Not with Grace.

Her fingers dug into my arm and she made me stop walking.

"I swear to God, if you don't tell me what is going on right now, I am yelling out that you're not wearing any underwear for everyone to hear." I gaped at her, but knew she was dead serious.

Shit.

I bit my lip and looked toward the field where the cheerleaders were warming up. Of course, Stella chose that moment to laugh at something Midori had said, her face lighting up. So gorgeous.

I opened my mouth.

"Not here. I can't do it here." So Grace and I went back to my car.

The doors shut and I was having trouble breathing.

Grace reached out and took one of my hands.

"Before you say anything, I want you to know that you can tell me literally anything and I will still love you. Even if you killed someone. No conditions, okay?" I squeezed her hand and forced the words to come out.

"I think I'm gay. No, I know I am." My entire body shook and I felt like I was going to die. Grace just started laughing.

"Yeah, and I'm black. What else is new?"

Did I hear her right?

"What?" I said and she stopped laughing.

"Oh, Kyle. I know you. How long have we been best friends? I've known for a long time. Maybe forever. I was just waiting for you to tell me." Words deserted me. I just kept opening and closing my mouth. Grace leaned forward and pulled me into a hug.

"It's not a surprise and it doesn't make me think any differently of you. How could it? You're you and I love you." Before I knew it, I was crying onto her shoulder and she was holding onto my shaking body.

"Oh, Kyle, I'm sorry this is so scary for you. I can't imagine, but I'm here for you. Whatever you need." Apparently I'd chosen well in my best friend. She rubbed my back and let me cry it out. I didn't even know why I was crying that much, but I finally got a hold of myself and pulled back. I'd gotten Grace's shirt all wet, so I popped open the glovebox and pulled out some napkins. I handed a few to her and used a few to blow my nose and wipe my face.

"So that happened," I said, laughing a little.

"Yup. It did. How does it feel?" I wasn't sure. My heart was still pounding, but I didn't feel any different. A little better, maybe. Because now someone other than Stella knew.

Stella.

We were very late for the game, but I knew that I needed to fix things with Grace first.

"You can ask," I said because I knew she would. Anyone would.

"Ask what?" she said and I rolled my eyes at her as I crumpled the napkins up and threw them in the backseat.

"How I figured it out, am I in love with you, that sort of thing." She snorted.

"You've already told me a ton, so I don't need to know anything else unless you want to tell me and I know you're not in love with me. Not that way." Lottery. I'd won the Best Friend Lottery.

"Oh. Okay," I said. She wasn't going to push, which was kind of a first for her. And totally at odds with the fact that she'd dragged me up here in the first place. Weirdness.

"Do I look like a hot mess?" I asked and she used some of the napkins to wipe the rest of the tears from my face and told me when my face wasn't red anymore.

"Your eyes are little puffy, but there's not a whole lot you can do about it. It'll go down. Just say that you had an allergy attack if anyone asks." Yeah, that wasn't going to work. I wish I had ice or some cold spoons or something, but it couldn't be helped.

"Come on," Grace said, getting out of the car. I took a breath and opened the door. She strung her arm through mine and we walked together back toward the football field.

"Where have you been?" Paige asked as we took our seats again.

"Robbing a bank," Grace said, putting the hood on her jacket up. It was a chilly night and I was wishing I'd brought gloves. The cheerleaders had their pants on tonight, but Stella still looked great. She looked good in anything. And probably nothing.

Grace nudged my arm and I looked over at her.

"What?"

Her eyes flicked to me and then where I'd been staring. At the cheerleaders. I looked away as fast as I could, but the damage was already done. Now Grace knew I was into a cheerleader. I just didn't want her to find out which one.

But she didn't drag me back to the car to grill me about it. She just turned back to the game and started clapping as our team scored a touchdown.

And my eyes slid back to Stella.

———◆———

Grace didn't say anything else after the game, but gave me a huge hug and told me that if I wanted to talk, she was always there. And that she loved me. I almost cried again, but made it home without losing it.

I feigned a headache and went to my room, but I spent my time lurking around the gayer parts of Tumblr. I discovered there were a lot of people in similar situations and I stayed up late reading through stories. For the first time since everything had started, I felt like I could take a deep breath because there were people who had been through the same thing. I could feel myself nodding as I read the posts. And I'd told Grace and the world hadn't ended. She didn't hate me, or think I was a freak, or not want to be friends with me anymore.

I wasn't crazy and I wasn't alone. I clicked out of Tumblr and texted Stella. She'd caught my eye a few times at the game, but we hadn't said a word to each other. But she'd texted me about an hour after and we'd been talking off and on the whole night. Nothing earth-shattering, just stupid little things and memes and jokes. Still, every time my phone dinged with a new message, my heart tried to smash its way out of my ribcage.

I hadn't told her about Grace. Mostly because I didn't know how she would react. If she'd think that I had outed her, or something. That would kill me if she thought that.

You can bring some movies, if you want. Or we can see what's on Netflix.

I cringed at how stupid it sounded, but I didn't want us to spend the whole day being awkward in my living room. I still had some fear that our chemistry would suddenly die and there would be nothing left for us to talk about.

Movies with girls making out?

Whoa.

Maybe? Do you have a lot of those?

I could almost hear her laughing.

Maybe . . .

I wasn't sure if that was a good idea or a bad idea. Or both.

CHAPTER 10

Stella

I didn't get much sleep that night, and when I finally woke up the next morning, I couldn't resist bouncing out of bed. I hadn't been this giddy in a while. It was like being ten again and going to my first concert.

I did my hair extra carefully, hoping that by the time I came home, it would be messed up from having someone's hands running through it. I also wore my favorite jeans that made my butt look great and a simple tunic with a t-shirt underneath. Casual, but cute. Or at least I hoped so.

I had a moment of panic just before I pulled into Kyle's driveway.

Was this a date? Were we dating? Was that what this was? We hadn't talked or used any definitions. Fuck.

What were we doing?

I was still flipping out as I walked to the front door with a pizza, a bag of chips, and sodas and rang the doorbell. She opened it with a grin on her face.

"Hey," she said, a little out of breath.

"Is this a date?" I blurted out and her smile fell.

"Um . . . Do you want it to be?" she asked. I opened my mouth.

"I have no idea." She laughed and pulled me into the house.

"Let's not worry about that now, I'm starving." That broke the ice a little as she led me into the kitchen to get out plates and so forth.

"How's your day been so far?" I asked, cringing at the terrible small talk.

"A little manic. I've cleaned the house within an inch of its life." I looked around and it was definitely cleaner than it was last time, not that it had been dirty or messy. Just lived-in.

"You didn't have to do that," I said, touching her arm as she popped open the pizza box.

She turned and her mouth was so close that I couldn't resist giving her a kiss. We were almost exactly the same height, so no one had to bend in half.

Kyle smiled as I kissed her and then stroked my face.

"I was trying to impress you. You're intimidating. You also look, really, really good today," she said and I couldn't help but grin. There was nothing like a compliment from Kyle to make me feel like I could conquer the world. Or at least a few countries.

"Thanks," I said, running a few strands of her hair through my fingers. She'd worn it down and I hoped it was for me. She'd also dressed up, or at least as "dressed up" as Kyle got with a nice pair of jeans and a short-sleeve button up that was white with pale green stripes.

She looked amazing.

"Is this a date?" I asked again.

"I don't know yet," she said, kissing my cheek and then turning her attention back to the pizza.

We both filled our plates, grabbed sodas, and put the chips in a bowl.

"Look how healthy we are," Kyle said as we both sat on the couch, putting our plates on the coffee table. Sitting at the dining room table would have been weird and too formal.

"The pizza has sauce on it, which is made from tomatoes, which are fruit. And potatoes are vegetables," I said, pointing to the chips. She laughed.

"Good point."

———————◆◆———————

We started out sitting with several feet of space between us, but when we were done eating, we'd somehow slid until we were sitting right next to each other.

"Hey," she said, bumping my shoulder.

"Hey back," I said, turning to face her. "What are we doing?"

She took a breath and shrugged.

"I don't know. I mean . . . do you want to talk definitions? It seems a little early for that. And weren't you the one who, two days ago, didn't want to label anything? Just wanted us to be two people hanging out and having fun in secret?" I opened my mouth to argue, but she was right.

"Well, I guess I changed my mind," I snapped and she laughed.

"There's the bitch queen," she said, but it didn't sound like an insult. It sounded more like an endearment.

"Shut up," I said, fighting a smile. "I don't know. I just . . . it's not enough. I feel like I want to have some sort of claim on you, which is totally ridiculous, but I can't help it." I hated admitting that to her. How much I wanted her.

"Wow," she said, blushing.

"What? Does that scare you?" She bit her lip and shook her head slowly.

"No. Because I kind of feel the same way about you. And it's crazy. This is crazy, Stella. We kissed for the first time less than a week ago. I thought you didn't even have a heart less than a week ago. It's not supposed to happen like this." How was it supposed to happen? It also wasn't every day that a girl fell for another girl. Maybe that was it. Maybe girls were just different. I didn't know, I'd never felt like this before. Not even about Shannon.

"It doesn't matter if it's supposed to be this way or not. It is what it is. And I like it. Like you." She snorted.

"Somehow I like you too. In spite of seeing you act like an asshole for years." I mean, I hadn't been mean to anyone. Just cold. Just closed off. Protecting myself.

"I don't get why you want people to hate you when, if they knew you like this, they wouldn't." I pressed my lips together. I had strong feelings for Kyle, but I definitely wasn't going to talk about that. Not this soon. Maybe not ever.

"I get that you don't want to tell me, but it still has me puzzled. Anyway," she said, waving that off and grabbing the remote.

"What do you want to watch?" she said, turning on the TV. I wanted to talk some more, but she'd clearly shut the door on that conversation for now. I guess she was probably still a little new to all of this anyway. I'd had years to deal with these feelings and she'd just started.

So I looked at the TV as she scrolled through Netflix. I thought about asking her if she wanted to watch *Blue is the Warmest Color*, but that movie had a ridiculously long and graphic sex scene between the two girls, so probably not the best idea at the moment. It was also kind of a pain because of the subtitles.

"I'm fine with whatever." I realized I didn't know a lot about Kyle. What movies she liked, music, what she did when she was home alone in her room.

"Okay, then you don't get to complain about what I choose. That's how this works," she said, scrolling through until she found what she wanted.

"Are you serious?" I asked.

"Yup," she said as she selected *Tangled*. I'd never seen it.

"You're such a dork," I said as she turned up the volume and sat back happily.

"Yeah, but you like me so what does that say about you?" Good point.

"Is there singing in this one?" I asked and Kyle gaped at me.

"You've never seen this? What is wrong with you?"

"Um, I'm not six years old?" Kyle rolled her eyes.

"You don't have to be a kid to appreciate Disney. Besides, the animation they had to do for her hair is worth watching alone." I knew it was a Rapunzel retelling, but not much beyond that.

"Okay, okay, if you say so," I said.

"You're going to like it," she said taking my hand and kissing the back of it."Promise."

She didn't let go of my hand for the entire movie.

"So?" she asked as the credits rolled.

"So, what?" She used the hand not holding mine to pinch my shoulder. "Ow!"

"You liked it. I know you did because you smiled and laughed." There was the cutest smug smile on her face. Made me want to kiss her.

"Fine. I liked it. Happy?"

"Ecstatic," she said, letting go of my hand and getting up to clear away the pizza stuff. I helped her bring everything into the kitchen and couldn't help myself from standing directly behind her and putting my arms around her waist as she rinsed off the plates.

She gasped a little and one of the plates clattered as she dropped it.

I pressed up against her so there was nowhere for her to go. So slowly, she turned in the circle of my arms until she was facing me. She swallowed and I couldn't stop staring at her mouth.

My fingers clutched her shirt and I leaned in the few inches between us to kiss her. Her hands, wet and soapy, gripped my head as I kissed her harder. She returned the force and I thought my knees were going to give out. Good thing I was holding onto her.

I pulled back just a little and was pleasantly surprised when she shoved her tongue into my mouth and dug her nails into my scalp. Sometimes I thought that the desire was one-sided, or at least that I wanted her more than she wanted me, but she was showing me that she definitely wanted me back.

My blood pounded in my ears and I couldn't breathe and my heart was going to explode. It was terrible and wonderful at the same time.

She finally pulled back, shaking a little. Kyle pressed her forehead against mine and licked her lips.

"I keep thinking that it's going to stop. That I'm going to kiss you and it's going to suddenly feel wrong and that I've made a mistake. But then I touch you and all the doubts are gone. Fuck, Stella." Her voice shook when she said my name and I brushed her hair back from her face.

"I feel the same way," I said and she dropped her hands from my head and neck to my shoulders.

"Sorry about the wet hands," she said, and I felt the wet spots on my shirt.

"Doesn't matter. I'd rather make out with you than have dry clothing." She laughed and I reached up to stroke her hair again. Kyle really had great hair.

She giggled.

"That sounded dirty." That started me laughing and I leaned forward to rest my head on her shoulder.

"This is really nice," Kyle said, moving her hands up and down my back. "I didn't know it could be this nice with someone. I thought maybe I was broken, or that I just hadn't met someone I was attracted to yet. A late bloomer." I nodded and kissed her neck. She shivered and I couldn't resist using my tongue a little.

"Stop it," she said, but her tone told me she didn't want me to do that. I laughed.

"You know you like it," I said and she made a little sound in the back of her throat that turned me on so much that it was painful.

"I do, that's the problem. I like it way too much. Your tongue makes me stupid." I barely understood what she was saying as I moved up and softly drew her earlobe between my teeth.

"Fuck, Stella." I wanted to make her say that again. And again. And again.

Her fingers dug into my shoulders and then she was suddenly gone.

It was just . . . too much. Too much of a good thing. Not a good thing. The best thing. So good it hurt. I couldn't handle all of that at once. It was like I'd been asleep my entire life and had been blasted awake by a tornado of color and sound and feeling.

I didn't know it was even possible to feel like that in every cell of my body. I needed some air. I couldn't take it.

Stella looked at me and I realized she'd thought I didn't want her.

"I just needed a break. When you do that, it makes me want to do a lot of things that I'm pretty sure neither of us are ready for at this particular moment." I ran shaking hands through my hair and she nodded.

"I understand. We shouldn't get carried away until both of us are ready for . . ." she didn't finish. A few weeks ago the thought of having sex with a girl would have been something I would have scoffed at and said I was not interested in at all. Now it was at the forefront of my mind and I couldn't see straight for thinking about it.

"Uh huh," I said, still finding it hard to breathe.

"We should –" she started to say, but her phone went off. She went back into the living room to get it.

"What's up?" I asked, following her.

She shook her head and set the phone down.

"Nothing. Just Midori wanting to know if I had plans tonight." She sat back down on the couch and I sat as well, but kept plenty of space between us. Neither of us could keep our hands to ourselves otherwise.

"Oh," I said. "You can go, if you want." She shook her head again.

"No, it's fine. I want to hang out with you." My heart got all warm and gooey when she said that.

"Where does she think you are?"

"Home, probably. Not sure. I don't tell her where I am every hour of every day. Where does Grace think you are?" I opened my mouth and then shut it.

"Hanging out by myself, I guess." And there was the problem. No matter how much chemistry we had, we couldn't ignore the fact that we were lying to everyone. Not even lying. Hiding. As if we were ashamed. I wasn't, that definitely wasn't it. I just had no idea what would happen if my parents walked in right now and found me holding hands with Stella on the couch. And I wasn't ready to find out.

"It's okay, you know. Keeping things like this. I don't want to force you to do anything. Especially since I'm not willing to tell anyone either," she said with a sigh, combing her fingers through her hair.

"This is going to get more complicated," I said, which was one of the reasons I hadn't wanted to talk about it earlier. But it was inevitable.

"I'm not a fan of hiding things, but . . ." she trailed off. There was no easy answer.

"We could just start making out again. We're really good at that," I said, and a smile lit up her face. I loved those smiles because I was pretty sure not a whole lot of people got to see them on a regular basis.

So beautiful.

"Mmmm, if we do that, then I might not be able to control myself," she said, slinking across the couch toward me.

"What if I don't want you to?" I whispered as she straddled my lap. Her fingers pushed back my hair and she smiled.

"Then I won't."

"You should. One of us should be able to say no." I clearly wasn't very good at it.

She laughed low and sweet. Fuck.

My hands rested lightly on her hips. If she shifted just a little, we would be in quite a position.

"Where's the fun in that?" she asked, and then did rolled her hips against me in a way that made me nearly black out. A moan escaped my mouth and she was very pleased with herself.

"Not fair," I said, digging my fingers into her hips. She bit her bottom lip.

"Never said I was going to be," she whispered, lowering her face to kiss me.

And then my parent's car pulled into the driveway.

I nearly threw her off my lap in my haste to put as much distance between the two of us as possible.

"I thought you said they weren't going to be here until later!" Stella hissed as she got up and tried to fix her clothes and hair. There wasn't a whole lot she could do.

"They weren't supposed to!" I hissed back and then grabbed her arm. My plan was to hide her in my room, but there was a huge hole in that plan because her car was in the driveway.

"Calm down," I said, putting my hands on her shoulders. "They won't think we're doing anything if we don't make them think that we're doing anything. We're just two girls hanging out. I should have told you to bring homework to make it more authentic." Stella swallowed and sat back down on the couch way over on one side and I sat on the other, turning the TV on. I took a few deep breaths and tried to calm my pounding heart.

"I'm sorry," I said before my parents came through the door.

CHAPTER 11

Stella

Well, I hadn't planned on meeting Kyle's parents. Ever, really. I mean, I knew who they were because everyone here knew everyone else's parents, but this was a completely different situation. I swore they could hear my pounding heart when they called out to Kyle and she said she was in the living room.

They both came around the corner at the same and weren't surprised to see someone else in the living room with her.

"Oh, hello," her mom said. Her parents were young and Kyle definitely resembled her dad more than her mom, who was willowy and blonde. Kyle's dad had her hair and was a little shorter than his wife.

"Mom, Dad, this is Stella. She's my partner for that English project and we were just finalizing our oral presentation," Kyle said and I almost choked on air when she said the world "oral." There wasn't anything she could say that would not make me think of sex.

"Oh, how nice," her mom said, beaming and coming over to shake my hand. I shook her father's as well. Guess he was the quiet one.

"Yeah, well, I should probably go. My dad wants me home for dinner." It wouldn't hurt to start laying groundwork to show them that I was a good influence.

"Of course, of course," Kyle's mom said before Kyle walked me to the door. I wanted to kiss her more than I wanted to take another breath, but that definitely wasn't going to happen.

"Oh, hey, do you have that book for me?" Kyle said, her hand on the doorknob. Her parents hovered a discreet distance away. Kyle gave me a look that they couldn't see.

"Yeah, it's in my car," I said, understanding what she was saying.

"Cool, I'll just come get it," she said, loudly and we both headed out the door.

"I wasn't going to let you leave without kissing you," Kyle said as we walked toward my car.

"My parents are totally watching right now, but . . ." she said, trailing off and jerking her chin at a particularly thick and high bush that happened to be right next to my car and blocked us from view of the house.

"Come here," I said, grabbing the hem of her shirt and pulling her to me. She stumbled and nearly fell.

"I got you," I said and she smiled before our mouths touched.

"Thanks, babe," she said and I got that little thrill.

"Anytime," I said as she left little short kisses on my lips, like she couldn't stop.

"I'll see you on Monday. Text me," she said, stepping away from me, still holding my hand. I tugged to make her stop.

"Wait! If you go back in there without a book, they're going to be suspicious." Her eyes went wide.

"Shit, you're right."

"Give me a second." One of the upsides of having a father who was obsessed with literature was that you never wanted for reading material. I always had a few paperbacks in my car, just in case I got stuck somewhere.

I looked through my backseat and found a copy of *War and Peace*. I smiled and handed it to Kyle. She raised her eyebrow at it.

"What?" I asked.

"Really? Have you actually read this?" What was she talking about?

"Of course. Several times. I had a summer of Tolstoy a few years ago." Kyle snorted.

"Summer of Tolstoy," she said, looking at the back cover with a little smile.

"Yeah," I said, wondering what she was thinking. But then she took a breath and looked up.

"Talk to you later." She brushed one finger along my cheek and then turned to walk back into the house.

If this were a movie, it would start raining and I'd run after her and pull her into a passionate kiss that somehow didn't leave both of us drowning or with hair in our mouths.

I sighed and got in my car and shut the door.

This wasn't a movie.

I'd told Midori I didn't want to go out, but that was because I'd thought I was going to be with Kyle until late, so now I was stuck. Unless I just wanted to sit in my room, read, and text Kyle. That didn't sound too bad, but when I got home Gabe called.

"Aren't you supposed to be out getting wasted and not talking to your little sister?" I asked.

"I'm going to a wine and cheese party later. I'm classy as shit." I snorted and sat down on my bed. Dad was in his office grading papers. As usual.

"I'm pretty sure classy people don't use the word 'shit', Gabe."

"Anyway, what's new with you?" I opened my mouth to tell him everything about Kyle, but then I slammed it shut. Hard enough to hurt my teeth.

"Nothing, really," I said, trying to make it sound as casual as I could.

There was a pause.

"Now, if I was an idiot, I'd believe that. But sadly for you, I'm not an idiot, so why don't you tell me what's really going on." For a second, I thought about hanging up on him and then just never answering his calls again, but that wouldn't really work when he came home for Christmas.

"Just school. They're up our asses about college applications already." That was a terrible excuse and I knew he wasn't going to buy it.

"Try again," he said. He was patient and would wait all night if he wanted to. I'd been down that road with him before. He was much better at it than I was.

"It's nothing, Gabe. Let it go." I didn't want to talk to him about Kyle. I didn't want to talk to anyone about Kyle. Part of me liked keeping her as a little sexy secret, even if it wasn't going to work, or was unhealthy for both of us. Sooner or later, someone was going to notice and hiding would only be sexy for so long before it got old.

"Star. You know you can talk to me about anything. You know if you told me you killed someone, I'd be in my car and heading to help you hide the body. Always." I knew it. I knew he loved me. I knew that love came without conditions, but telling him was just . . .

"I can't," I said, my voice breaking. "I just can't."

He sighed.

"Oh, Star. I wish I could be there for you right now. I can tell you're going through something and I wish I could be your big brother in person and help you slay those dragons." I laughed. When we were little, Gabe used to pretend to read to me, but all the stories he told me were ones he'd made up, with me as the main character. It was no wonder he was in college for writing, but I always thought he would become a novelist instead of a journalist. Maybe someday he would.

"Yeah, I know. But I can deal with this. I'm a big girl." I'd be heading off to college in less than a year. And I'd never been someone who needed to be coddled. Not having a mom growing up might have something to do with it, or maybe it was just me.

"Even big girls need help sometimes." I hated that he was right.

"Who do you go to when you need help?" I asked.

"Dad," he said. "Or you. You're really good at giving advice. For a girl." I snorted. He didn't mean it.

"Yeah, I know."

"Why don't you talk to one of the girls on the squad? Midori?" I wish. But this was definitely something I wouldn't talk to them about unless it was a last resort. Gabe would be most likely, and I still couldn't do it.

"This isn't the kind of thing she can help me with."

"Hmmm . . . Then I don't know what to tell you. Can't give me even a tiny hint?" A tiny hint would give it all away. There was no subtle way to say "I like girls and one in particular."

"No," I said. "Look, can we talk about something else? How's school?" I thought he would protest, but he started talking about his classes and the articles he was doing research for. Gabe's passion was feature articles, where he could get in-depth with one subject. He always sent me his articles and they were brilliant. He was going to win a Pulitzer someday, I swear.

I got off the phone with Gabe and headed to the kitchen to get something to eat. The pizza had been a long time ago. Just as I was rummaging through the freezer for something easy, my phone dinged with a text.

I'm sorry about my parents. Again.

Kyle.

It's NBD. You didn't know they were coming home. It's fine.

It was cute how bad she felt. At least she heard the car before we'd started making out again. Having her parents catch us in the act would have been . . . Well, I didn't even want to think about that.

I miss you. Is that weird? Sorry if that's weird.

So adorable.

If you're weird, then I'm weird because I miss you too. I'm just having dinner now.

I found a bag of pasta with chicken and shoved it in the microwave.

What are you having?

I told her and then asked what she was eating. That led to a somewhat heated discussion about olives, (terrible or delicious) guacamole, (terrible or delicious) and beets (we both agreed they were terrible).

I liked learning those little things about her. The things that not everyone knew. I wanted to know them all. I wanted to know what song she had stuck in her head. I wanted to know her most embarrassing moment. I wanted to know what side of the bed she liked to sleep on.

I wanted to know it all.

Midori texted me again to ask if I was sure I didn't want to go out and I said no again. I was too busy texting with Kyle. It was so much easier than actually taking face-to-face or on the phone.

She started sending me silly selfies and I sent a few back and we had a whole section of the conversation that were just emojis.

I really, really liked her.

She was funny and sweet and I couldn't believe I hadn't seen it sooner. How could this amazing girl have been there all along? Was I that self-absorbed?

Probably.

The last message she sent me had a kissy emoji and two words.

Goodnight, babe.

On Sunday I was forced to do all the homework I'd ignored on Friday night and Saturday, along with listening to my parents go through all they'd learned about financial aid at the seminar.

Riveting stuff.

I could feel my eyes glazing over and the words were going in one ear and out the other. Basically, I had to apply for any and every scholarship I could, stay in state and maybe sell an organ or two.

My parents had been scrimping and saving my entire life, but it still wasn't going to be enough. I hated it for them and I planned on getting at least two jobs this summer and stashing away as much money as possible to pick up the slack. They shouldn't have to pay for *my* education. At least not all of it.

Stella was probably going to have no problem. Seeing as how her dad taught and I knew they had more money than my family. Whatever. It didn't matter. She had her situation and I had mine.

Thinking about college just reminded me that it was happening in less than a year. Things with Stella were . . . complicated already. Neither of us knew what we were doing, or if anything was going to come of it. How could anything come of it? We'd not only have to both come out and hope everyone accepted us, but then deal with going to different colleges. There was just no way it was going to work out.

I guess I should just stop worrying about the future and just think about now. About how I wish we were making out instead of me sitting here and listening to my mom explain the FAFSA form.

I was about to head to my room when something my mom said made me stop in my tracks.

"So, who is that girl, Stella? She doesn't seem like your kind of friend." Ouch. But I knew what she meant. Stella looked like a princess and I looked like the stable-hand or something.

"Oh, we're just working together in AP English. That's it." I shrugged and tried to slip away to my room, but my mom was giving me a look. Uh oh.

"It's just that you don't invite a lot of people over. We hardly even see Grace." That was true. I didn't like subjecting my friends to the nuttiness of my parents.

"Well, we had to work on the project, so . . ." I trailed off. Dad was still staring at the forms, but Mom was giving me one of those looks where you knew she knew you weren't telling the whole story.

Shit.

"Okay, well, I'm going to do my homework." I gave her what I hoped was a normal smile and headed off to my room.

I sat on my bed and wondered if I should text Stella. I was really terrible about keeping this secret and it had only been a couple of days. I'd make a horrible secret agent.

I'd told Grace and now my mom knew something was up. How long would it take everyone else?

The thought made my stomach churn.

I picked up my phone and texted her.

I think my mom knows. She was asking about you and I am pretty sure I'm a terrible liar.

Her response took a few minutes.

I mean, it was bound to happen, right? Guess it was just sooner. What did you tell her?

This was different than Grace knowing because now Stella was involved. Revealing my secret meant revealing hers and that made me feel sicker than anything.

Just that we were working on a project. I tried. I'm so sorry.

Kyle, it's fine. I know you didn't do it on purpose. We just have to be more careful. Or tell people. Those are the only options.

Two options; I didn't know if I could handle either of them.

———————◆————————

On Monday it was so hard not to kiss Stella when I walked by her in the hallway. She glanced at me, but didn't give me a smile. I tried to keep my face neutral, but I couldn't help but be happy to see her.

Grace was talking in my ear, but all I could see in the crowd was Stella. She passed me and it was so close that she just barely brushed my hand with hers. I shivered.

"Are you even listening?" Grace said, grabbing my other arm and stopping me.

"Yeah, sorry. I was just off in the clouds," I said, refusing to look over my shoulder to see if Stella was still there.

"Uh huh," Grace said and pulled me into the bathroom. We were going to be late, but something told me she didn't care.

"Is this about what we talked about on Friday? I wanted to give you some space this weekend, but maybe I shouldn't have?" I had been sort of surprised that she hadn't texted me, but I'd been so wrapped up in Stella I didn't really notice. It made me feel like a shitty friend.

"No," I said too quickly. Grace crossed her arms and leaned against the wall as if she was going to stand there all day and wait for me.

"It's not about that. Not exactly. Things are just . . . a little weird. Because I always thought I was straight," I said the last part in a whisper, even though we were the only two in here at the moment.

"Yeah? I bet. Are you having second-thoughts?" About my sexuality? Oh, hell no. Definitely 100 percent gay. Gay, gay, gay. Lesbian. Whatever.

"Nope. I know that it's right and that it's true." Grace opened her mouth as if she was going to ask me how, but then shook her head.

"You want to know how I know. I know you do. If the situation were reversed, I'd want to know. But I can't tell you that. Just that I do." Her eyebrows drew together and we stood there in silence for a while.

"I'm sorry, Grace. I don't like keeping secrets from you. I don't like keeping them from anyone, but I need you to trust me on this one. Please?" She bit her bottom lip and sighed, putting her arms around me.

"I know. I'm sorry. I just hate that you feel like there are things you can't tell me. But of course I trust you." I rested my chin on her shoulder for a second and thought about how different hugging Grace was than hugging Stella.

Two different galaxies.

"I promise that if/when I tell someone, you'll be the first. Okay?" She let me go and nodded.

"Okay. And if you need a friend to go to the Pride Parade, I'm your girl. I mean, your heterosexual girl," she said, giving me two thumbs up. I laughed and we headed off to class.

Stella and I headed to the library again during English class.

"This worked out in our favor, didn't it?" she asked as we sat next to each other. I was starting to think of this corner as our place. Or one of our places.

"Totally," I said, kissing her cheek. She wrinkled her nose in the cutest way and then kissed me on the lips.

"No tongue," I said into her mouth. She pulled back and pouted, which made me laugh.

"I love your tongue, but it makes me forget everything and that's probably a bad idea to do in a place where someone could catch us," I said and she moved away from me.

"Yeah, you're right. So tell me more about how it went with your parents." I told her and that made me want to tell her about Grace.

"I'm worried you're gonna hate me," I said as I handed off the bag of gummy bears. I'd made sure I had some when I left for school today.

"Why would I hate you?" Stella said, running her fingers up and down my arm, causing goosebumps.

"Because I told Grace I was gay." The fingers stopped and I couldn't look at her face.

"How did that happen?" Her voice was level, so maybe she wasn't going to be pissed?

"Basically I was ignoring her at the game and she made me go back to my car and tell her what was wrong. She's not really good at letting things go." I looked up at her and she had a neutral expression on.

"So I basically broke down and told her. I didn't say anything about you, I swear, but today she talked to me about it again and I think she's on high alert for any lesbian behaviors. Like me not being able to stop staring at you." She gave me a half-smile.

"Well, you're not the only one who's guilty of that. I would stare at you all day if I could." I loved it when she said things like that.

"Anyway, I just . . . I'm really bad at this secret thing and I just wanted to let you know that I might do something that is going to out us." Both of us.

She sighed and looked down at her nails. They were polished in a soft grey today.

"It's not your fault that you suck at lying, I guess. And our friends and family would be pretty stupid if they didn't notice at least some change." She took a breath. "I think my brother knows. Or at least suspects."

She'd talked to me about her older brother, Gabe, who she absolutely idolized. It was so sweet and I was a little jealous, being an only child.

"Yeah?" She nodded.

"He's really perceptive, but he hasn't pushed me or anything. If I told anyone, I'd tell him. Or at least I'd tell him first." I nodded.

"I hate that we feel like we have to lie. I mean, we *shouldn't* feel this way," I said. Stella gave me a sad smile.

"It's just the way things are right now. They've changed a lot. At least we're probably not going to get stabbed or spit on, but who knows? There are still plenty of homophobes in the world." I bet there were. It wasn't something I'd given a lot of thought to. Until now, of course. Now it was something I had to consider.

My mind was starting to spin again.

"Hey," Stella said, squeezing my shoulder. "I'm not going to lose you again, am I?"

"No. I just . . . I was thinking about homophobes and that got me thinking about a whole lot of other shit. There's a lot to this liking girls thing, isn't there?" Stella scooted over and put her head on my shoulder.

"But there's a lot of good things too." I rested my head on hers. That was true. It wouldn't be worth doing if there weren't more pros than cons.

"Should we make a list?" I said, almost as a joke.

"Let's do it."

She laughed a little and I decided her laugh was number one.

"Girls are prettier," Stella said.

"Girls smell better."

"Girls are better listeners."

"Girls have better boobs."

That one made us both laugh.

"Boobs are pretty fantastic. How did I not notice?" I said, looking down at my own chest.

"Yours are really nice. In case you were wondering," Stella said. "But don't get a big head about it."

"Why, Stella, that's the nicest thing anyone's ever said to me." She smacked my shoulder.

"Shut up."

"Girls have better nails," I said, taking her hand and stretching her fingers out.

Stella was just about to reply when the bell rang, shattering our little bubble. We both got up and it was almost painful to walk away from her.

We would text later, but it wasn't the same. I just wanted to be with her. As much as I could. Basically all the time. Being with her was like breathing fresh air for the first time and it was so hard to let go. I hoped it wasn't going to keep getting harder.

CHAPTER 12

Stella

I was totally off again at practice on Monday night and coach was not pleased. I kept messing up simple choreography I could do in my damn sleep. It was so bad that she pulled me aside.

"Is everything okay? Everything at home or in class?" Everyone else had headed to the locker room to change or had left, so it was just the two of us in the gym.

"No, I'm just tired," I said. I figured it was a good enough excuse. "Or maybe I'm coming down with something." Mysterious illness was another good one. Maybe I should have said I had PMS.

Coach put her hand on my shoulder and did that thing that adults do when they sort of lean down and look deeply into your eyes as if they're going to decipher all your secrets with one look.

"I'm fine, Coach. Promise." I gave her a smile and she pulled me into a hug.

"You let me know if you need absolutely anything. You got it?" I hugged her back and thanked her. I was all gross and I just wanted to go home and take a shower. I grabbed my stuff and headed out the door, taking my hair down and running my fingers through it. I was thinking about other things so I didn't notice that someone was standing beside my car. It was almost dark, but not so dark that I didn't recognize who it was.

"What are you doing here?" I said, nearly dropping my bag in shock.

"Um, waiting for you and feeling like a creepy stalker?" Kyle said, crossing her arms in the cold. I was still overheated from practice so I didn't have my coat on.

"Do not tell me you've been standing out here for hours, because that might veer into stalker territory." I unlocked my car and threw my duffel in the back and shut the door, walking over to where she was leaning against the driver's side.

"Yeah, no. I definitely didn't do that. I went home and did homework and thought about you and figured I would come and bring you a little pick me up." She held out a bottle of green juice and a paper bakery bag.

"What's in there?" I asked. She smiled.

"Open it and find out." I moved so I was under the streetlight and opened the bag. A chocolate croissant.

"Because the green juice and the croissant cancel each other out. Calorie-wise," she said, pushing her glasses up on her nose.

"You know that's not how it works, right? I thought you were supposed to be the smart one." She snorted.

"See if I do anything nice for you again." I reached out and took her hand.

"I love it. Thank you. And I'm really happy to see you. Even if I'm all gross." Kyle laughed and pushed some of my hair over my shoulder. We looked more alike now, with me in sweats and with my hair all messy.

"You are so beyond gross right now," she said, and demonstrating by pulling my face forward for a kiss. It was quick, because we didn't want anyone to see us.

"Thank you for the croissant. And the juice." I kissed her cheek and squeezed her hand again.

"You're welcome, babe." She let go of my hand and headed back to her car across the lot.

"Girls are more thoughtful," I yelled after her and she gave me a thumbs up.

"Definitely!"

I ate the croissant first and had the juice second, but I was still starving when I got home, so I made myself some dinner.

"How was practice?" Dad asked.

"Good," I said, which was what I always said.

"And how's your presentation?" I froze in the act of putting together my salad.

"Good," I said again.

"Are you going to give me any more details than that? I thought we'd passed this phase a few years ago." He leaned against the counter.

"It's good. We're basically done and we made the changes you suggested. We're ahead of everyone else, so we've been using our class time for studying." Studying, cuddling.

"Good, good. And how's it working out with your partner?" I'd told him the bare minimum about Kyle. And now I was starting to get suspicious.

Were the two of us wearing neon signs on our foreheads advertising that we were hanging out together? Or did we just have very perceptive people around us?

Or was I just paranoid?

"Fine," I said, for some variety. "She's actually really cool." I could talk about Kyle as a friend without raising too many red flags. Because his assumption wouldn't be that Kyle and I were into each other.

"That's nice. It's good to make new friends. I mean, friends that are more into academics." I gave him a look.

"You're saying Midori isn't into academics?" I asked. "She's a National Merit Scholar." He sighed and looked at the ceiling. He was more than used to debating with me.

"That's not what I meant and you know it. I like seeing you branch out and meet new people. Why don't you have her over sometime?" Um, I'd already done that and it had ended in me kissing Kyle. But my house was a better place for the two of us to hang out, if only because my dad was gone so much.

"Yeah, maybe I will. She'd probably like to get out of her house. Her parents are a little obsessive and hovery," I said and cut it off there because I was saying too much.

"Is she an only child?" He crossed his arms and smirked.

"Yes, as a matter of fact she is." We both laughed.

"I can understand that. You only want what's best for your kids and sometimes it's easy to go a little overboard." I finished making my salad and started pouring on the olive oil dressing.

Dad came over and stole a cherry tomato before I could swat his hand away.

"I'm glad you didn't hover. I mean, not like that. They're constantly checking in with her, making sure she's happy and healthy and everything." I started eating while standing up because I was still so hungry.

"She'll be grateful for it one day, I'm sure." I had no idea if she would or not. Would I even know Kyle down the road? I didn't like thinking about the future that far ahead. I was so focused on college that I couldn't really see beyond that. Everything else was blurry.

"Uh huh," I said as Dad drifted back to his office to burn the midnight oil.

"**Y**ou're all glowy today," Marcey, one of the vet techs said on Tuesday when I was at the vet clinic.

"I am?" I asked, putting one hand to my cheek.

"Yeah, you look really happy lately. Could it be because of a boy?" There it was. The assumption that all girls were into all boys. My face froze and I shook my head.

"Nope. Guess I'm just getting a lot of sleep or something." She got distracted from replying by the entrance of one of our problem clients, Rufus, with his owner Geoff. Rufus was already howling and whining and practically dragging Geoff out the door. It took three of us to get Rufus into the exam room so Dr. Cope could give him his vaccinations for the year.

You know what I hate? The assumption that all girls like boys.

I texted Kyle when I got home, after I'd showered and was toweling my hair off.

Same. It's the default and it's stupid. I mean, MOST girls like boys, but not all.

Not us.

I liked talking about her and me as one unit. Neither of us was close to being ready to call us something like girlfriends, but I did like thinking of us as . . . something.

Gal pals.

Yeah, no way. That was stupid. Maybe we needed to make up a new term.

Nope. Not us. That's another one for the Pro list. We're unique.

You mean "not normal"

I wasn't sure if she was being sarcastic or not.

Do you really think that? That we're not normal?

I waited and waited for an answer, but then she just ended up calling me.

"No, I don't think we're not normal. That wasn't what I meant," she said without any preamble.

"What did you mean?"

She sighed.

"I don't know, Stel. I don't know. I didn't mean it. I'm sorry. That came out completely wrong. I was more talking that other people would think that. Not me." I moved my hair over one shoulder.

"I know. I know you don't think that. It just caught me off guard, I guess. I'm sorry I got a little defensive." She sighed.

"No, I'm sorry that I said it. Typed it. Whatever. Ugh, why is this all so complicated?" It sounded like she'd slumped on her bed.

"We don't have to make it complicated. We could always end it. Go back to our regular lives. Try and be straight again." I was joking about the last part and she laughed a little.

"Yeah, I think I'll pass. Also, I like making out with you too much to give that up."

"Same."

There was a beat of silence and I sat back on my pillows.

"What are you doing right now?"

"Just sitting in my room and praying that my parents won't barge in and give me more practice essays for scholarships. I already had to do one today." Sounded awful. And she didn't need practice. She was smart already.

"I'm sorry. You could always sneak out of your house and come over to mine." I wasn't serious, but I almost wished she would do it. Just show up and stay with me.

"Yeah, my parents would definitely notice if I was gone. They have a security system. But I would if I could. Would it earn me extra points in the romance department?" I smiled.

"Maybe. You earned some today when you showed up after practice." She laughed.

"Good to know. I'm trying to out-romance you."

"Oh, so it's a competition is it?"

"Yup, and so far, I'm totally winning." I scoffed.

"Yeah, so far. But I'm pretty sure I can beat you."

"Oh yeah?"

"Yeah."

She heaved a little sigh.

"I miss you. Even though you're on the other end of the phone. I wish you were like, sitting next to me. Could you sneak out? That would earn you some romance points." I chewed my lip. I mean, hypothetically I could. Dad was knee-deep in work and left me to my own devices.

"But how would I sneak in if your parents have an alarm system?"

I could hear the smile in her voice.

"I go to bed after they do. I'm the one who sets it."

I sat up.

"Are you serious right now?"

"Why not?"

I opened my mouth to argue.

"I don't know," I said and got up. "Give me twenty minutes."

Kyle

I didn't think she'd actually do it. I totally expected a text saying *nevermind*, but then my parents went to bed and I didn't set the alarm and went to my room to wait. Fortunately, my house was a ranch style, so my bedroom was on the first floor. Although, if I'd been on the second floor, it might have been interesting to see her try to get up there. I imagined a trellis would somehow be involved.

But then, almost exactly twenty minutes later, there was a soft tap at my window.

I skipped over and pushed it up, finding a smiling Stella on the other side.

"I can't believe I'm doing this," she whispered as I helped her scramble through the window and into my room.

"I can't believe it either," I said, not letting go of her. She stepped forward.

"So do I get romance points?" she asked, a smirk on her face.

"Definitely," I said, giving her a kiss. She laughed and we tumbled onto my bed together, tangling our limbs. Her hair was still a little damp from her shower earlier.

"This was such a good idea," I said as she kissed me with desperation. I kissed her back just as hard, both hands fumbling with her clothes. She just had a sweatshirt on with a pair of yoga pants and they were both driving me crazy.

"Such a good idea," she said, just before she drove her tongue into my mouth. I moaned and she somehow flipped us so she was on top and I was flat on my back. Her fingers tangled in mine, raising them over my head.

"Fuck, Stella." She pulled back only to bite my bottom lip and laugh.

"I love it when you say that. It turns me on so much I feel like I'm going to die."

"You saying that turns me on so much I feel like I'm going to die," I said as she looked down at me, her hair falling. I wanted to push it out of her eyes, but my hands were already occupied.

"I should have put my hair up," she said, sitting up and letting go of my hands so she could pull a hair tie off her wrist and put her hair back in a ponytail.

"I'll remember that for next time," she said before she attacked my mouth again. She stole my breath and made my bones turn to warm caramel and I'd never felt anything so good. I tried to pull her closer, but I couldn't get her close enough. My glasses were smashed to my face but I didn't want to take them off because then she'd be all blurry.

"More. I want more," I said into her mouth and she laughed.

"Are you sure?" she said, looking down at me with swollen lips.

"Yes," I said, the word more breath than substance. Stella cupped my face with both hands and kissed my forehead. Instead of ramping up, she slowed us down, laying kisses across my entire face until I was trembling under her, my fingers digging into her sides. She didn't seem to mind. Or notice.

Her lips skipped over my jaw. I made a sound of frustration and she smiled against my skin and just barely kissed my chin.

"You said you wanted more. I'm giving you more, babe." I took a deep breath as she moved further down. To my neck where the skin was sensitive and her kisses made me see stars.

My blood pounded in my ears as she reached the neck of my t-shirt and pulled it down just enough so she could kiss the top of my collarbone. A breath hissed through my lips.

I wanted her to take my shirt off. I wanted her to take everything off and I wanted to take her clothes off and do everything, but a very quiet voice in the back of my head said that wouldn't be a good idea.

Not yet.

Not tonight.

So I shifted under her so she'd look up.

"My turn," I said, crossing my legs around hers and rolling us over again. She squealed a little, but the change in position was definitely nice.

"Oh, I like this," I said, looking down at her, laid out on my bed.

"God, you're beautiful." The only light in my room was moonlight that spilled in through the window and it lit up her hair and made her eyes look mysterious.

"Thank you. You're beautiful too, Kyle." I sighed.

"We can argue about who's prettier, or you can let me kiss you."

"Fair point." I laughed as I kissed her forehead and gave her the same treatment she gave me. She held onto my arms as if holding on for dear life and she unconsciously thrust her hips into mine.

I was going to lose my mind.

We were both completely clothed, but I was so fucking close to coming that I didn't know what to do.

I tried to focus on kissing Stella. Doing whatever I could to get her to make those little whimpering sounds in her throat. I was gentle, because neither of us needed a hickey because then there would be questions. We didn't need questions.

I tasted the underside of her jaw and the pulse on her neck and the hollow of her throat. It was good. It was all good.

So much different than any of the times I'd kissed a boy. I didn't even know what those had been, but this was something else entirely. I was never, ever, going to kiss a boy again. Like ever.

I stopped kissing her, just so I could watch her.

"What are you doing?" she asked, looking up at me.

"Watching you. I don't get to do it that often when I won't get caught. Or when it's okay." I ran one finger from her forehead, down her nose and to her chin, down her neck and stopped just at the top of her sweatshirt.

I could tell she wasn't wearing a bra and I wanted so much to shove my hands under her shirt and feel them. Feel her nipples against my palms.

"Kyle?" she asked. I had been very obviously staring at her chest.

"I was just thinking about touching you. Here." I skipped my hands over her boobs and she arched up into me.

"I want you to," she said, her words uneven.

"I think . . . I think we should slow down." The words sliced me to say, but I knew that we were very close to stepping over the edge.

"I know you're right, but I seriously hate you right now. I'm not getting to sleep anytime soon." Me neither.

I climbed off her and sat on one side of my bed, with her on the other. We were both still breathing hard.

"How did you get here?" I asked. Probably a little belated.

"Drove my car without the headlights until I got far enough from the house. And I parked a few houses down so your parents wouldn't get suspicious. I think we're fine," she said, taking down her ponytail that had gotten a little messed up, and combing through her hair with her fingers.

"I was thinking what we'd say if we got caught. And then I decided we just shouldn't get caught," I said.

"Solid plan." The air between us cooled a little, which was probably a good thing. I still could barely think of anything other than her, but at least now I was keeping my hands to myself.

"So this is your room," she said, looking around. It was small, but cozy. I'd done what I could with the space and fixed up furniture from yard sales and discount stores.

"This is where the magic happens. And by magic, I mean me and my hand. Sometimes both hands." She snorted and rolled her eyes.

"Perv." I gave her a look.

"You can't tell me you don't."

She fiddled with her hair.

"No, I do. Doesn't everyone?" Pretty sure. Unless they were too uptight or something.

"We probably shouldn't talk about that right now anyway," I said and she nodded.

"You okay?"

She sucked on her bottom lip.

"I've just been thinking about . . . about next year and college and how all of my plans basically went out the window. Thanks a lot, asshole." She found a shoe on my floor and chucked it at me. I caught it and tossed it back on the floor.

"Why is it my fault? What did I do? She rolled her eyes.

"You're irresistible." I tried to hide a smile.

"I'm sorry?"

"You should be. Asshole." She got up and came to sit next to me again. I put my arm around her shoulders and she leaned into me.

"I don't like that I can't see you whenever I want. That we can't just do this without hiding," she said. I rubbed her shoulder because I didn't have a good answer.

"Well, Grace took things really well. Maybe you could try Midori? Or your brother?" She stiffened.

"I'm scared," she whispered. "I'm scared they won't love me the same way."

"Oh, babe. You know that's not going to happen."

"But it could. It could." Never let it be said that Stella Lewis wasn't stubborn.

"You're right. It could. But that would mean they didn't love you enough in the first place. Because if this is the thing that makes them love you differently, then that love wasn't that strong anyway. Okay?" She sniffled and I moved her so we were facing each other.

"I wish it wasn't like this," she said as I brushed her tears away with my thumbs.

"Shhhh, it's okay. It's okay, baby." I kissed her and she melted into me, letting me hold her. It was a different kind of kiss than earlier. A softer kiss. Something more like comfort than desire.

"Do you want me to come with you?" She shook her head.

"No, that would definitely not help. Because then they'd look at you and assume we were together." Right.

"Or, you could tell your brother on the phone and I could be here and hold your hand. I wouldn't say a word," I said, pretending to zip my lips shut.

She thought about that.

"Not right now. But maybe this weekend. Maybe. I don't know." She took both of my hands.

"I should probably go. I really don't want to risk getting caught and the longer I stay, the better the chances are that we will." She kissed both of my hands and then my lips.

"Goodnight, babe. Drive safe," I said as I walked her to the window.

"Thanks." With one last kiss, she was out the window again and I went to set the alarm.

CHAPTER 13

Stella

Kyle had planted the seed of the idea of telling Gabe in my head and it was starting to grow. I imagined all the potential scenarios and went over them with Kyle on Wednesday when we were in the library together.

"Okay, what is your absolute worst case scenario?" Kyle asked as she tossed gummy bears into her mouth.

"Um, him telling me that I'm going to burn in hell, that he's never talking to me again, and that he's telling Dad. That's pretty much the worst." Kyle raised one eyebrow.

So. Fucking. Cute.

"Don't do that, it makes me want to kiss you." She started wiggling her eyebrows up and down and I couldn't stop laughing.

Of course the librarian chose that exact moment to come around the corner in search of who was destroying the peace of her library.

Kyle and I froze. Fortunately, we hadn't been in a compromising position.

"If you two are just going to come in here and goof off, I'm going to send you back to class. Don't make me tell you again." Since we were sitting, she was a lot more imposing. Especially when she wagged her finger at us.

"Of course. Sorry," I said, trying my best to look contrite.

"We won't do it again," Kyle said, moving her leg so it hid the bag of gummy bears.

"It better not." With one last glare, she turned on her heel and marched off to do whatever she did all day.

"Whoa, that was close," Kyle said, picking up her gummy bears again. "No more laughing. Or smiling." She made her face devoid of emotion and it was so ridiculous that I started giggling and slammed a hand over my mouth to muffle the sound.

"You're not supposed to be doing that," she said, shaking her finger at me.

"Shut up. You have to stop or else I'm going to laugh again."

She heaved a sigh.

"Fine."

"**H**ey, I feel like I haven't seen you in forever," Midori said on Wednesday afternoon as we headed to the locker room to change for practice.

"I know, I've just been really busy," I said, my mouth going dry. It was a bad excuse. I'd been using most of the time I usually spent on Midori with Kyle and sooner or later, something was going to have to give.

"Yeah, I can tell. Busy with what?" She set her bag down and whipped her shirt over her head. She already had her sports bra on underneath. I turned my back and fiddled with my bag, grabbing my clothes.

"Just . . . school. I've been stressing about college. And I've been working more hours." I pulled off my shirt, unsnapped my bra and traded it for my sports bra and a tank top. I didn't turn back around until I was covered again.

Midori was standing with her arms crossed and her eyes narrowed. "Uh huh."

I groaned and sat down on the bench where I'd put my bag.

"What do you want from me? Do I have to tell you every single fucking detail of my life?" A few other girls passed by and gave me weird looks, but went to change.

"Whoa, no one said that." She sat down next to me and I could see the concern on her face.

"What's going on with you? Are you okay? You've just seemed different lately." Guess Kyle and I were perfect for each other because neither of us could hide anything.

"It's just . . ." For a second, I almost blurted it out. But I couldn't tell her before I told Gabe. That was the new plan and I was going to stick to it.

"Can you come over on Sunday? Or maybe we could do something on Saturday night?" That would cut into my time with Kyle, but both of us had been neglecting our best friends and there had to be a way to balance the different parts of our lives and still see each other.

"Yeah, sure. You want to maybe grab some pizza? Just the two of us?" We hadn't done that in so long.

"Absolutely." I gave her a smile and she patted my shoulder before grabbing her cheer shoes and slipping them on.

Guess I was telling two people this weekend.

It was like being on a train that wasn't slowing down.

Kyle. I had to remember I was doing this for Kyle. And for me. Hiding this part of myself hadn't been fun. Each time someone talked to me about having a boyfriend or a husband or anything like that, I felt like a liar. It made me feel awful and honestly, even before Kyle I'd been sick of it. But I told myself I could hold on until college.

Not anymore. I'd had enough, and it wasn't just about her. I was tired of not being able to be myself. To be scared of myself. I didn't want to do it anymore.

I had a weirdly good day at practice, nailing my tick-tock heel stretch three times in a row. I was feeling good when I walked out to my car and there she was again.

"I figured we could make this a thing," she said, handing me a juice (mango, this time) and a glazed donut.

"It should definitely be a thing, thank you," I said, giving her a quick kiss and looking around. There were a few cars still in the lot from other cheerleaders and teachers working late.

"I decided I'm going to tell Midori," I said as we sat in my car and I split the donut in half, offering it to her.

"Oh, yeah? How are you feeling about that?" She took a bite and I licked the glaze off my fingers.

"Good? I guess? I wanted to tell her today because she sort of cornered me, but I want to tell Gabe first. And that probably means I should tell my dad soon. I don't want to make Gabe keep that secret from him." She nodded and we munched on our donut halves.

"Grace is still watching me. I think she knows that I have a thing with someone, or at least a crush and she's taken it upon herself to find out who. Oh, and she's also started pointing out cute girls. She's really taking this ally thing seriously." I laughed. I couldn't picture Midori taking things that far.

"I think you'd like Grace. And she would like you. Once she found you weren't actually a raging bitch." She grinned at me and I wiped some glaze from the corner of her mouth and licked my finger off.

"But I've been so careful to make her believe that. Wouldn't want to ruin things now." Her eyebrows drew together.

"I still don't get it. Why you're so different with me and like that with everyone else. I'm guessing you're not like that with Midori." No. Not completely. She got to see bits and pieces of my real self, but Kyle was the only one, outside of family, who saw me. Just me. Unvarnished and real.

"You wouldn't get it," I muttered and shoved the last bite of donut into my mouth.

"Oh, that's nice, Stella. You're literally the only person I can talk to about liking girls, but I 'wouldn't get' what you're going though. Yeah, okay." Her words hurt, but not enough to make me tell her the reason why.

"Look, it's my thing. Can you just drop it?" I knew exactly what was going to happen when I said those words, but it didn't stop me from saying them.

I expected Kyle to tell me to go fuck myself and slam the door, but she didn't. She just sat there and waited.

"I know what you're trying to do. You're trying to be a bitch to make me leave, but too bad, because I don't believe you. So I'm just going to sit here." She crossed her arms, as if she really meant business.

Damn. I'd underestimated her. And her bullshit tolerance when it came to what I could give her.

"Fine, do what you want to do." The words didn't come out as forceful as I wanted. I gripped the steering wheel to have something to hold onto and smeared leftover donut glaze on it. Great.

"Stel," Kyle said, touching my shoulder, but I jerked away from her.

"You don't even know me. Just because you've had your tongue in my mouth and we've talked a few times, doesn't mean you know me." I couldn't stop the words from coming. I was just so used to curling in on myself and going on the defensive before someone could hurt me.

I had to hurt them first.

"Good effort. I'd give it an eight out of ten," she said, giving me a smirk.

"What the fuck is wrong with you?" She shrugged one shoulder.

"I like you. And I'm not all that sensitive, I guess." I opened my mouth to say something else, but short of screaming at her, or throwing her out of my car, she didn't seem to be budging.

"You are weird." She grinned.

"Never claimed to be otherwise."

I fought a smile and lost.

"Ha," she said, a little sound of triumph. "I win."

"Brat," I said, smacking her in the shoulder.

Somehow she'd defused the situation and got me to smile. No one else had done that before and I didn't know what to do with it.

"But I'm your brat. You know you like it." I did. Too much.

"Anyway, I'm going home. But I'll text you later." She smacked a kiss on my cheek and was out the door, heading to her car.

I shook my head and started my car.

Kyle

I was definitely going to have bruises when this phone call was over. It was Saturday and I was next to Stella in her bedroom, holding her hand as she prepared to call her brother.

"He's probably busy," she said, staring at her phone. "He probably won't even pick up."

We'd been going through this same thing for a while now, but I wasn't going to force her before she was ready. Grace had sort of put a gun to my head and I didn't want that for her.

"We don't have to do it today," I said. She shook her head.

"No, it has to be now. Because I'm going out with Midori later and I promised myself I'd tell Gabe first." With a nod of her head she hit send for his number and raised her phone to her ear.

I was sitting so close that I could hear it ringing.

He picked up on the third ring.

"Hey, Gabe," she said, her voice a little shaky. I couldn't hear what he said in return.

"No, I'm fine. I just . . . There's something I need to tell you. Do you have a minute to talk?" She waited and then took a deep breath. We'd practiced what she was going to say all week.

"Dad's fine. No, I didn't get kicked out of school. Can you just shut up for a second?" She took another breath and somehow squeezed my hand harder. I wouldn't be surprised if she snapped one of my fingers. Damn cheerleading muscles.

"Gabe, I'm gay." Her entire body shook with the words and her hand trembled in mine.

You got this, I mouthed at her, but she was too busy with Gabe.

"No, I'm sure. Yes, I'm serious. No, I haven't told Dad. You're the first." Second. Technically.

She opened her mouth to say something else, but Gabe must have been talking.

"Shut the fuck up, you did not know," she said, letting go of my hand.

"No you didn't . . . No . . . No, Gabe . . . Stop it . . ." Okay, was it going bad or . . . ?

I was dying to know what he was saying. I wished she'd put him on speaker.

"I'm not going to say that because you did not know before me. You're just saying that because you want to be right." She rolled her eyes, so that was a good sign.

"Look, I'm not fighting with you about who knew I was gay first. The bottom line is that I am and I like girls and Dad doesn't know yet, so don't say anything. I'm going to tell him. Probably tomorrow." Wow. Her brother, Midori, and dad all in one weekend. She was better than me.

"Oh my God, Gabe. Yes, I did kiss Shannon. No, I do not have a girlfriend." She gave me an exaggerated wink and I had to muffle a laugh.

"Okay, I'll tell you when I get a girlfriend so you can do your brotherly thing and interrogate her to figure out what her intentions are. Okay. I'll talk to you later, jerk. Okay, bye." She set the phone down on her bed and I pulled her into a hug.

"I'm still shaking," she said and I could feel it.

"I'm guessing it went well? From what I could hear." She snorted into my shirt.

"Yeah, you could say that. He basically said that he's known for years and doesn't give a shit and just wants me to be happy." She sat back and pulled her knees up.

"I mean, I *knew* that was what he was going to say. I know my brother. But I still was scared out of my mind. My heart is pounding." She put her hand on her chest and let out a little breathless laugh.

"I think I need a drink now."

Since we couldn't have an alcoholic beverage, we had seltzer water with maraschino cherries in it.

"Too bad I don't have any cherry stuff or we could have made Shirley Temples," she said as we sat in the living room.

"How do you feel now?" She set her drink down on a coaster and shrugged.

"The same? I guess I thought I would feel different or something. But I'm still me. Still gay." I laughed.

"Lucky for me."

She gave me a half-smile that made my heart do flips.

"I'm really proud of you. For doing that."

"Thanks," she said, looking down at her hands. Stella painted her nails every week without fail. They were painted a cute mint green.

"Hey, would you do my nails?" I asked. She looked up.

"Yeah, sure. I can do your toes too."

"Cool." She skipped off and came back with one of those clear plastic containers and it was filled to the brim with polish. There had to be at least fifty or more bottles.

"Polish much?" I asked when she set it down on the coffee table with a clunk.

"It's fun. Something to do." She shrugged and set out the supplies and I scooted closer, flattening my hand on her thigh.

"That's not going to be distracting at all," she said, lining up the bottles of polish for me to choose one.

"I have no idea what you're talking about," I said, pointing to the same color polish she was wearing.

"This one?"

"Yeah, I want us to match." She beamed. How cute.

"Okay," she said, unscrewing the top of the polish and starting on my pointer finger.

"Can I run a hypothetical situation past you?" I asked as her head was bent over my hand to make sure everything was perfect.

"Sure."

I took a breath.

"What if I told my parents and you tell your dad and your brother already knows and our best friends will know so . . . what would you think about us maybe telling more people? Or, if not that, just . . . hanging out? In public?" More and more, I was learning that I was willing to risk/give up a hell of a lot of things to get more time with Stella. I'd do just about anything for more time with Stella.

She looked up as she finished my first nail.

"Hypothetically?" she asked, raising one perfect blonde eyebrow.

"Hypothetically."

She put the brush back into the jar of polish.

"I think . . . I think that I'd be okay with that." I exhaled shakily.

"Really?" She took my polish-free hand.

"Really." Stella lifted my hand to her lips and kissed the back of my hand like she was from an old movie or something.

"So you'd be willing to hold my hand in public and go on dates outside of either of our houses? Hypothetically." I felt like I had to keep adding that.

"I'd be willing to pretty much go anywhere with you, Kyle. In case you didn't know that," she said, twisting her fingers with mine.

I loved the idea of being out with her, our hands entwined, walking together.

"It wouldn't bother you to be out with me?" She shook her head.

"No, why?"

"Because I am easily defeated by stairs. And if we were chased by a murderer, I'd probably end up dead." She stared at me for a second and then it hit her. My limp.

"Oh! Oh, no. I guess I don't see it as something that's bad or wrong, or whatever. It's just you. And I like you. All of you." That was something I'd definitely considered when it came to dating, but I'd figured I would just find a guy in college, since colleges were generally liberal places. But it had still been in the back of my mind.

"I won't always be able to keep up with you." I started to say something else, but she shook her head.

"I like *you*. Whatever form you come in. The packaging isn't important. And I happen to think your packaging is perfect." I bit my lip and looked down at my nails again.

"Thanks."

"You wouldn't feel weird about being out with me?" she asked, going back to painting my nails.

"No. When I really think about it, no. It feels right. Sometimes I look at you and I wonder how I ever could have thought I was straight." She giggled.

"Yeah, I feel the same way sometimes. But I haven't been 'straight' for a long time."

I rolled my eyes.

"Okay, okay, you win. You knew before me." She looked up.

"It's not a competition. You got there in the end. And there are some people who go almost their entire lives without figuring it out."

"I guess you have a point."

"I do." Stella concentrated on my nails and I watched her work. It wasn't an uncomfortable silence. Just the two of us being together. She finished my first hand and I blew on my nails as she worked on my second hand.

"We'll have to do another coat," she said after she'd finished the first. I waved my hands in the air to dry them.

"Want me to do your toes while you wait for those to dry?" she asked. I slipped my socks off.

"As long as you don't think my feet are ugly," I said before I put them in her lap.

"Aw, your feet are cute. Cuter than mine. My second toes are longer than my first and I hate it." I bet it wasn't that bad. Maybe I'd ask if I could do her toes. Not that I was great at nail polish. I just didn't use it that much because it chipped after two seconds.

I was glad she couldn't see my leg, because I wasn't ready for her to see all the surgery scars. Most of the time I didn't think about them, but I definitely didn't want to when I was with Stella.

"So, you're going to tell your parents?" she asked as she finished my second toe.

"I think so? I mean, it went well with Grace and you told your brother and I think it'll be okay. I hope it'll be okay. I just hate feeling like I'm hiding something from them. As much as they drive me crazy, everything they do is because they want the best for me. And they've sacrificed their entire lives to see that I didn't grow up like they did." Both of my parents had had rough childhoods. They hadn't given me a lot of details, but I knew enough. And I could read between the lines.

"That's sweet."

"Yeah. Bottom line is that I know they love me. And if they love me, they have to love all of me, right?" She nodded.

"Exactly."

CHAPTER 14

Stella

I was second-guessing my choice of venue for my talk with Midori that night. It meant that anyone walking by or eavesdropping would hear what we were talking about. Fortunately, there was a booth tucked into a corner near the kitchen that the waitress seated us at and if I spoke low enough, no one would hear.

"I wonder if she thinks we're on a date," Midori said after she'd taken our drink orders.

"What?" I said, nearly choking on my water. I felt all the blood drain from my face.

"I just said what if she thought we were on a date. It was a joke. I wasn't serious." That didn't stop me from shaking. But this was Midori. My best friend. The girl who had had my back. Literally, in some instances at cheer practice.

"Oh, yeah, right," I said, pretending to laugh, but probably sounding deranged.

We talked about what to order and homework and the new stunt our coach wanted us to try.

I was trying to figure out how best to tell her when I just blurted it out.

"I'm gay," I said as she picked up the first slice of pizza. The waitress had just left us, so we were alone.

Midori froze.

"I'm sorry, what?"

"I'm gay. That's what I didn't want to tell you." She set the slice of pizza down on her plate and opened and closed her mouth a few times.

"Okay." She picked up her napkin and set it on her lap and started to eat.

"That's it?" I asked. She wrapped a string of melting cheese around one finger and then put it in her mouth.

"Is there more?"

"I guess I just expected you to have more of a reaction." She smiled and took another bite of pizza.

"I mean, I think I sort of knew, but it doesn't change who you are. I don't see you any differently. And you're my best friend. So that's it." Oh. Okay?

I opened and closed my mouth a few more times and Midori laughed.

"Stella, it's not a big deal to me. I know that there are some assholes out there, but I'm not one of them. If girls are what you want and they make you happy, then that's what I care about." Well.

"Wow," I said and she shrugged one shoulder.

"Do you want to talk about it? Or not talk about it?" she asked. I finally picked up a slice and bit into it.

"If we didn't have to talk about it that would be great. I feel like it's all I've thought and talked about for weeks and I'm a little bored to be honest." We both laughed.

"Okay then. So, what do you think about fundraising online for the new uniforms? Because car washes are so overdone and I really don't want to wash a car in a bikini so some gross old guy can ogle me." I made a face.

"Totally agree." So we talked about fundraising for cheer and how we couldn't wait for this year to be over and the ridiculousness of college application essays.

It was amazing.

Before she left, I gave her a huge hug.

"Thank you for being my best friend," I said.

"Anytime," she said, hugging me back.

Two down, a bazillion to go.

———————◆———————

I was on such a roll that when I got back on Saturday night from hanging with Midori, I sat Dad down in the living room and told him.

He just sort of blinked at me and told me he'd known since I was five or something.

"You're my daughter. It's my job to know you." He smiled and gave me a hug. I started to cry a little and he held me and told me that he loved me.

"I thought this was going to be horrible," I said, wiping my eyes. He kissed the top of my head.

"Why? Why would you think that this would change the way I see you?" I didn't know for sure.

"I'm really proud of you for trusting me with this, Star. And I know that you'll be happier when you can live openly as yourself." My stupid heart kept swelling due to these amazing people I had in my life.

"So you're not going to disown me or take me to 'pray away the gay' camp?" I asked, totally joking. He shook his head.

"You know, it always fascinates me that when people are having a child, they say 'we don't care what we have, as long as it's healthy' but if that child turns out to be gay, or transgender, suddenly that's not good enough." I nodded and we sat down and did what we always did and had a lively discussion of gender and heteronormativity and he even gave me a list of books that he'd read. My dad had read a little bit about almost everything, so he always had a ready book recommendation. If you needed a book on pangolins, he'd have a title ready and waiting in his brain to give you. Sometimes he made me feel stupid. But he'd had more years of reading under his belt than I had.

So that was Gabe, my dad and Midori down. The three most important people (other than Kyle) in my life. Everyone else? I kind of wished I didn't need to tell them. Why was the pressure on me?

I texted Kyle because I needed to talk to her.

So Midori and Dad were fine. NBD.

Wow! That's awesome. I'm telling parents tomorrow. Might call you sobbing and ask if I can come live with you if things go badly.

Aw, I wished I could go and hold her hand. Or even do it for her. I was getting pretty good at it by now.

You don't have to, Ky. It can wait.

I know, I know. But I just want to get it over with, you know?

I did. I absolutely did. Now that my family knew, I almost felt . . . light? Like something that I'd been carrying for a long time inside me had lifted. It was nice.

I wanted that for Kyle too and I hoped beyond hope that she'd get it.

I'm here for you. No matter what. Okay?

Okay. I'll let you know how it goes. Goodnight, babe.

I sighed and set my phone to charge as I climbed into bed.

Everything and nothing had changed in just a few days. I guess I expected to feel more of a change in myself, but I felt the same, but better. The best word to describe it would be "quiet."

Maybe it was supposed to be this way. I didn't really believe in fate or that shit, but this felt right. The timing felt right. *Kyle* felt right.

My mom looked like she was going to die from a heart attack when I sat her and Dad down in the living room on Sunday afternoon. I had a whole speech prepared, with answers to any potential questions and I wasn't going to cry this time. I mean, I was going to try not to cry this time. No promises.

"Kyle, you're scaring us," Mom said, clutching Dad's hand. "Are you pregnant?" she said in a whisper.

And I burst out laughing. Oops.

"This is not funny at all, Kyle," Dad said, putting his arm around Mom.

"I'm sorry," I said, trying to stifle the giggles. "I'm really sorry. It's not funny. I mean, it is in the context." I bent over, my stomach aching.

"Kyle!" I straightened up and swallowed the rest of my laughter.

"I'm sorry. It's funny because I'm gay. As far as I know, two girls can't make a baby, so that's not something you have to worry about. Yay." I raised my hands and wiggled my fingers like jazz hands.

They both stared at me.

"You're gay?" Mom said. "You're not pregnant, you're gay?"

Uh oh.

"Yes?"

She let out a huge sigh and fell back against the couch.

"Oh, thank God. I thought it was something bad. I need a minute to get my heart back to normal." She put her hand on her chest and I looked at Dad.

"Well, thank you for telling us, but you didn't need to make a huge production out of it. We were both preparing ourselves for the worst."

"I'm sorry?" I said. What was going on here?

"It's okay, kid," he said, getting up to give me a hug. Mom joined him a second later and we had a family hug. I couldn't remember the last time I did that.

"We love you, Kyle. You're *our* daughter and we are beyond lucky that we got you." That made me cry. Guess I couldn't come out without crying. That was going to be really embarrassing.

"I love both of you," I said. "I know I don't seem like it sometimes, but I do. And I appreciate all of the sacrifices you've made for me and all that you do." Mom pulled back from the hug and held my face between her hands.

"If you think about it, we're even luckier because not everyone gets a gay child. You're rare. Like a diamond." She kissed my forehead and I cried some more.

After that, they sat me down and I told them that I'd recently come to realize these feelings and I could tell Mom wanted to say something.

"That Stella you had over is really pretty," she said, totally obvious. I felt my face go red.

"Are you two . . . ?" she trailed off.

"Um, kind of? It's very, very new. We've just been hanging out and stuff. She hadn't told her family either, so we had to do that before we could really, you know, move forward." Why was this so awkward to talk about? If Stella was a boy, it wouldn't be a big deal.

"Well, I think you should have her over for dinner so we can officially meet her. She must be pretty special," Dad said with a wink.

"Yeah, she is," I said, biting my lip. "She really is."

"You look happy, baby," Mom said, tears glistening in her eyes. "Really happy."

"I am. I think," I said. We talked more about life and whether or not I'd want to propose, or get proposed to, and how a wedding with two brides works, and it was the best conversation I'd had with my parents in ages.

It made me feel guilty about how often I brushed them off or shut them down or closed my door in their face. I vowed that I was going to stop doing that so much. Shutting them out of my life.

We had another group hug and then Dad said we should celebrate and go out to dinner, which we almost never did, so I went to put on one of my nicer button up shirts, black pants that didn't have rips in the knees, and my black Chucks. I even made some effort with my hair, got out the curling iron I'd bought on a whim years ago, curled the ends of my hair and left the rest down. I even did eyeliner and put some colored gloss on my lips.

"You look so pretty!" Mom said.

"Thanks." She gave me another hug and we headed out to the nicest restaurant in town. "Nicest" meant they had white tablecloths and tall candles on the table and had a huge wine menu.

I didn't get to text Stella until after we'd gotten home from dinner, and I bet she was climbing the walls to know how it had gone.

So Mom asked if I was pregnant. And then I laughed. And then I told them and she said "oh thank God. I thought it was something bad."

OMG! I can't believe it. So they were fine?

Uh, yeah. They were more than fine. Mom said that since being gay is rare I'm like a diamond or something.

WOW. That's . . . wow.

I know. So that happened.

What do we do now?

I wasn't sure. I was still reeling from the fact that my parents were all aboard the rainbow train.

Can we give it another week? Please? We had our presentation on Monday, which meant that after that, there would be no more private "study" sessions in the library and we'd go back to being on display all the time. It sucked, but I just wasn't ready to face everything else yet.

Sure. Whatever you need. BTW, I'm really proud of you.

I couldn't help but smile. Hearing that she was proud of me made my heart want to smash out of my chest.

Thanks. That means a lot. And I'm proud of you too. We both did a

lot this weekend, didn't we?
    That we did.

While Stella gave our presentation about feminism in *Jane Eyre* I couldn't take my eyes off her. If I hadn't liked her before, I probably would have when she started to talk. She was incredible. Smart, articulate, and beautiful. She absolutely nailed it and I could tell Mr. Hurley was pleased when I handed in our paper.

"Well done, ladies," he said.

I looked at Stella and held my hand up for a high five. She looked quickly around before she connected her hand with mine, ever so briefly. It took all my control not to grab her hand and hold onto it for the rest of the class. We had to sit through the rest of the presentations, which were mostly a snore-fest.

"Finally," Stella said when the bell rang and we were dismissed. I got up and expected her to go back to not wanting to be seen with me, but she packed up her bag and waited for me.

"Oh, are you going to walk with me?" I asked.

"Maybe," she said, her voice all flirty. Most everyone had already left, so we were pretty much safe, as long as we talked in a low volume.

"You gonna carry my books too?" I asked and she rolled her eyes.

"No, because this isn't a television show from the 1950s. Come on." I left the room first and she followed after me, keeping pace. I realized I didn't even know what class she had next.

"Where are you headed?"

"Calc. You?"

"Health." I made a face. It was the worst class ever. The gym teacher just stood up and told us not to have sex and talked about the different muscle groups. I pretty much slept through most of it, but it was a requirement for graduation and there was no way out.

"Well, I'll walk you as far as the health room," she said with a smile before looking around to see if anyone was watching us. As far as I could tell, no one was.

"Thanks," I said and she turned to look at me again. "You look really cute today, by the way. I wanted to tell you earlier." She ducked her head as we walked and blushed a little.

"Thank you. I hate that compliments from you turn me into absolute mush." I laughed.

"Well, that makes two of us." People passed by us and didn't even look twice. They were all dealing with their own shit and insecurities and thoughts. One good thing about teenagers; we were so absorbed with our own issues that we didn't notice other people's.

"So, what are you doing tonight?" I asked and she stopped walking.

"Are you asking me out?" Her voice was loud and I stepped closer to shush her.

"No, I meant that we should hang out. At your house or something. By the way, my parents want to meet you. Like, officially. Even though we haven't decided what the hell we're doing. They want you to come over for dinner." I cringed as I said it, but she laughed.

"Wow, meeting the parents. That's a big step, Ky. Is your dad going to bring his shotgun to the table and start cleaning it?" We were both definitely going to be late, but I didn't care. I slowed my pace even more and she did too. Like we didn't want to leave each other.

"Uh, I don't think so. Seeing as how he doesn't have one? And you can't get me pregnant, so there's that." She snorted.

"Yup. That's one thing we don't have to worry about. Should we add it to the list?"

"Definitely." We finally reached the health classroom and Mr. Varney was already trying to get everyone in order, which usually took at least five or ten minutes of threatening everyone with detention. He never actually gave them out because he wanted everyone to like him.

Adults were weird sometimes.

"Um yeah, you can come over. My dad might be home, but he'll be working and he's pretty shy so he'll leave us alone. Unless that's not okay with you?" Mr. Varney was yelling at someone and I hoped I could slip in while he was distracted.

"Yeah, that's fine, I guess. I'll meet him eventually, right? You want me to just meet you there at like five?" I knew when her practices got out now because she'd texted me her schedule.

"Perfect. I'll see you later. Babe." She whispered the last word and gave me a wink before strutting off to Calculus. I definitely watched her walk away.

I slid into my seat in the back of the room just as Mr. Varney was threatening Esther Wilson with detention for being on her phone already.

Phew.

I was flipping out a little as I drove to Stella's house. I'd brought green juice and Boston cream donuts for each of us this time. I wasn't scared of her dad, exactly, but knowing that he knew that Stella liked girls and her suddenly having me over looked a little suspicious. Or maybe I was thinking too much. Probably.

I took a breath and got out of my car with the bakery bag and the juices. I walked slowly so I didn't trip and drop anything. I made it to the front door and knocked, feeling like a weirdo.

"Hey," Stella said as she opened the door. "Come on in." I did, reluctantly, and she shut the door behind me. I pretended that I wasn't looking for her dad, but I totally was.

"Relax," she said in my ear. "He's already in his office." I shivered as she ran her hand down my back and then plucked one of the juices out of my hands.

"Thanks, babe." I followed her into the living room and she sat down. Her hair was still wet from her post-practice shower and she had a tank top and shorts on. I was pretty sure she was not wearing a bra under the tank top, which was a little distracting.

A lot distracting.

"How was practice?" I said, forcing myself to look at the juice as I unscrewed the cap.

"Good," she said, lifting her hair off her shoulder and draping it over the back of the couch. "I'm sore. Coach made me do a million scorpions and my back is mad." I had no idea what she meant. She must have seen the question on my face. She sighed and then got up. I had no idea what she was going to do until she took her foot in one hand and swung it behind her head.

Holy. Shit.

She popped her foot up until she was almost bent in half and then leg go, acting like people did that every day.

My mouth was dry as she sat back down.

"Who says cheerleading isn't a sport?"

"Not me," I managed to say. "Doesn't that hurt like hell? Your body isn't really supposed to bend like that. Unless you don't have a spine."

"You dork. I've been cheering since I was a kid. If you get flexible when you're young, it's easier. I barely feel it anymore, as long as I make sure I stretch every day." I just stared at her.

"What?"

"That was some contortionist shit right there," I said. She waved me off.

"Eh, everyone can do that." I shook my head.

"You're crazy." She grinned.

"Shut up and hand me whatever you have in there." I passed the bakery bag over to her and she pulled out the donut.

"Oh, helloooooo." She gazed lovingly at it.

"Should I leave you two alone?" I said, pretending to get up. She bit into the donut and rolled her eyes at me.

"I love carbs," she said through a mouthful of donut. I shook my head at her and pulled a napkin out of the bag and started wiping her face.

"Stop it," she said, pulling away. I was just about to tackle her against the arm of the couch when someone cleared their throat. I whipped around to find a man with graying blonde hair, glasses, and Stella's eyes looking down at us.

"Oh, hello Mr. Lewis," I said, putting distance between me and Stella and hoping that my face wasn't too red.

"It's nice to finally meet you, Kyle," he said. Right. Stella had already told him about me. I glanced at her and she was still staring down at her donut as if it was going to start talking for her.

He stepped over and put his hand out. I shook hands with him, feeling more awkward than I ever had in my entire life.

"I heard your presentation went well," he said and I could feel him trying to make conversation, but it was just making the whole thing worse.

"Yeah, Stella was amazing," I said and then wanted to kick myself.

"Whatever," she said, fighting a smile.

"What? You were. You were the only one who knew what they were talking about." I needed to stop right now, so I shut my mouth.

"Do you girls need anything?" he asked, shifting from foot to foot. He was nervous, which almost made me feel better about the whole situation.

"No, we're good, Dad. Thanks," Stella said, finally looking up. She was more than a little red and I had the feeling she and her dad were going to have a chat about me when I left. I didn't want to know.

"Okay, well, if you do, just let me know." He shuffled to the kitchen and made himself some instant coffee and then headed back to his office.

"So that was your dad," I said when I was sure that the door was closed and he couldn't hear us.

"Yup. That was my dad. And I'm pretty sure that I'm due for a lecture after you leave." I bit my lip.

"Sorry about that. I guess I got a little carried away. That seems to happen a lot around you." She couldn't hide her smile.

"I guess that's okay, because I feel the same way about you. But I definitely think that in the future when my dad is here, we should have at least two feet of space. Just . . . so we don't get carried away. It happens so fast." She was right, as much as I hated it.

I sighed and moved a little further away.

"Should we measure? Should we draw a line?" She crumpled up the napkin and threw it at me, but missed.

"I'm only protecting us from the horror of my dad walking in while we're in a compromising position. I would rather die than have that happen." Yeah, me too.

"I know, I know. All these rules," I said, taking my hair down. It was pulling at my scalp and I could feel a headache coming on.

"If you were a boy, he'd still have the same rules. Probably more." True. There was that.

"At least he didn't ask me if we were seeing each other," I said, shuddering. That would have been the worst. The "so what are your intentions with my daughter" speech. Ugh. I hoped I would never have to hear one of those.

"Yeah, but he will after you leave. What do you want me to tell him?" Since my parents knew about her, I figured it was only fair.

"You can tell him. I mean, he's going to find out anyway at this point, so lying would just be silly." And I knew he wasn't an idiot. Stella had gotten her smarts from somewhere.

"Yup. You're right."

There was silence as she finished the donut and I sipped my green juice.

"So, what do you want me to tell him? That we're seeing each other? That we're dating?" I tried to answer, but the truth was that I didn't know.

"I guess? I mean, for lack of a better, more accurate, term." She nodded.

"Do you think that at some day, you might want to call what we're doing dating? Or be up for calling yourself my girlfriend?" My heart fluttered when she said the word "girlfriend." I wanted that. I wanted to talk about Stella as my girlfriend. I wanted to introduce her as that.

Definitely.

But was I ready for that?

Was I ready for a girlfriend and all that came with it?

I didn't know. Not yet.

"I'll be totally honest with you: Yes. I want that, but I don't know if I can handle it yet. I hate being the one who's not ready because I feel like I'm holding you back, but I don't want to say yes, and then let you down. That would be worse." So much worse.

She reached out and took my hand. The one that still had the polish on it that matched hers.

"I don't want to push you or rush you into anything. I totally get it. This is all new and scary for me too. We'll get there. Because I like you and you like me and we're excellent at making out." I laughed as she squeezed my hand. I never knew hand-holding could be so awesome. I mean, seriously.

Awesome.

"Cool," I said, kissing the back of her hand.

"Want to watch a movie and hold hands?" she said and I nodded.

"Yeah."

So we did. I scooted a little closer to her, but still with enough room that if her dad came out again, we could play it off.

I let Stella choose the movie because I didn't really care. I just liked being with her.

She chose the newest movie with Rebel Wilson, which I was fine with because she was funny as hell. Plus, it let me watch Stella laugh a lot and that was pretty damn great too.

We held hands the whole time, even though they started getting sweaty. Stella's dad didn't come out, which was great. I wondered if he was hiding in there, wary of walking into something.

"Stop being so paranoid," she whispered in my ear as my eyes flicked down the hall to look at his office door.

"I can't help it," I hissed back.

"Stop it," she said and then her tongue was licking my earlobe and I stopped thinking about just about everything.

"Fuck, Stella, you have to stop. What if he comes out?" My eyes fluttered shut as she kissed down my neck. This girl was trying to kill me. In the best way possible. I'd happily die at Stella's hands.

"But that's the fun. The almost getting caught," she whispered against my skin as her hand crept under the hem of my shirt. Just the barest brush of her fingertips on my stomach nearly had me losing my mind.

"Seriously, Stella." My protests were getting weaker and weaker.

She laughed against my skin and her fingers kept working. I was dying. I was actually dying.

And then I nearly did when my phone vibrated.

"Shit," I said, reaching for it. My parents were calling, wondering where I was. I looked at the clock and it was five after nine. They were super strict about school nights. I mean, not that they really had to be. Until now, I guess. I'd always had a curfew, but they'd never had to enforce it.

"I should go," I said after I got off the phone with my mom. I'd told her that I was with Grace. I hated lying, but I didn't know if she'd approve of me hanging out with Stella now.

"Okay," she said, walking me to the door. I put my coat on and told her to say goodbye to her dad for me.

"I hate to say it, but you should probably meet him in some sort of official capacity." She cringed as she said it.

"You're probably right." Meeting the parents. Big step. For any relationship.

"I'll see you tomorrow after practice?" she asked. As if I needed a reminder.

"I hope so. Have a good night, babe." I wasn't sure if I could kiss her or not and then she grabbed my coat and pulled me in, capturing my lips with hers. We both kept our tongues to ourselves and the kiss was over far too soon.

"I wasn't letting you leave without my goodnight kiss," she said, tapping my nose.

"Bye, baby," she said as I opened the door.

CHAPTER 15

Stella

I did see Kyle the next day before she met me by my car. We just happened to be walking into the cafeteria at the exact same time. Totally unplanned. I was with Midori and a few of the girls from the squad and she was talking with Grace and Molly.

I had a brief moment of terror, but then she beamed at me and my heart did back handsprings.

"Hey," she said, as if we did this every day. My mouth was dry so I had to swallow before I could respond.

"Hey." Wow, amazing response. I was so good at this.

Grace and Midori were both watching us and the other girls had puzzled looks on their faces.

"Do you want to sit with us?" Midori said and I whipped around to stare at her. She just shrugged one shoulder.

"Um, thanks. We're good," Grace said, hiding a little smile. Kyle and I didn't hang out with the same people. It wasn't as if there was an impossible divide between us, but meshing our two groups didn't seem like something that was going to happen. At least not without a reason.

"Okay," I said, and started walking.

"Okay," I heard Kyle say behind me.

"That was a little awkward," Midori said in my ear. "Are you into her?" I gave her a look.

"Ohhhhhh," she said as it dawned on her. "Don't worry, I'll keep my mouth shut." We grabbed trays and got in line.

"What was that?" Courtney asked.

"What was what?" I said, trying to play it off.

"You talking to Kyle. Did anyone else get a weird vibe there, or was it just me?" Nope, wasn't just you, Courtney. Pretty sure everyone felt it.

"We got paired up in English for a project so we've been talking. She's nice," I said, hoping that would satisfy them.

"Huh," Courtney said and got distracted by a cute boy. As usual. Midori poked me in the back and winked. She was definitely going to want details later. Well, as many details as I could give her. There weren't a whole lot. I bet Grace was going to do the same thing with Kyle.

What had we gotten ourselves into?

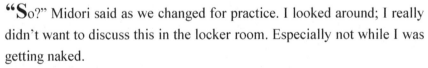

"So?" Midori said as we changed for practice. I looked around; I really didn't want to discuss this in the locker room. Especially not while I was getting naked.

"So, what?" I said. "I don't think this is the right venue for this discussion." I looked around and popped my shirt over my head and switched out my bra.

Midori huffed.

"Fine. But after practice, you're going to tell me. Because I definitely saw something going on there," she said in a sing-song voice.

"Shut up," I said.

"Hey, I'm not criticizing. She's cute. In a nerdy kind of way. Is that your type?" We were not having this conversation right now.

"I will talk to you later," I said through gritted teeth.

"Fine, fine. But we will talk." Guess I wasn't getting out of that one.

She winked at me and then skipped out of the locker room while I tried to get my shit together.

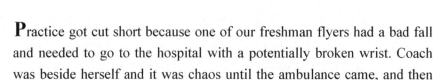

Practice got cut short because one of our freshman flyers had a bad fall and needed to go to the hospital with a potentially broken wrist. Coach was beside herself and it was chaos until the ambulance came, and then she left with Macey, so the rest of us rolled up the mats and headed home.

I took my time in the locker room and so did Midori until we were the only two left.

"Okay, it's just us," she said after she'd walked around and made sure we were alone. I sat down on the bench and she sat facing me.

"Is she your girlfriend?" was the first question.

"Um, yes and no. We aren't official, but I think we will be soonish. It's still weird and new and scary so we're taking things slow." I was absolutely fine with that. I knew Kyle thought she was dragging her feet, but I was happy with how things were going with us. I didn't want to rush and then fuck this up. I didn't want my first relationship to end in complete disaster. I didn't want to end it at all, really. But I couldn't think that far ahead. Not yet.

"Oh my God, that is so cute! I can't even deal with this." I gave her a look.

"You seem more excited about this than I am." She laughed.

"I'm just excited *for* you. Because I can see how much you like her. You look at her like you're falling in love with her. If you haven't already." I froze.

What?

I tried to make words come out of my mouth, but I couldn't. I was out of them.

"I wish you could see your face right now," Midori said. She looked like she was highly enjoying this. And I was ready to slide off the bench and onto the floor.

Falling in love.

Falling.

In.

Love.

What?

I wasn't in love with Kyle. I barely knew her. We weren't even dating, for fuck's sake. We'd only kissed a little. Okay, a lot. But we hadn't even gotten close to being naked. Or anything else.

Shit.

My mind started reeling and I could tell that I was starting to hyperventilate.

"Whoa, Stella, breathe." Midori clamped onto my hand and helped me calm down.

"I don't know what that was," I said, feeling cold sweat run down my back.

"I think that was you freaking out about Kyle. I'm sorry, I think I said too much." I shook my head and swallowed a few times.

"No big. I think you just blew my mind a little. And I need to sit here alone and think for a minute. If that's okay with you?" She got up and squeezed my shoulder, but left me alone.

One of the sinks had a leaky faucet and the dripping was driving me crazy. I got up and went to turn it all the way off and stared at myself in the mirror. My face was all shiny from sweating during practice and my hair was a mess. I pulled it out of my ponytail and then put it in a bun on the top of my head.

Like Kyle's.

I couldn't stop thinking about her. My fingers dug into the porcelain of the sink.

I wasn't going to think about what Midori had said. I wasn't going to think about the feeling I'd had when she said it. Nope. I wasn't.

Once I'd finally gotten a grip on myself, I threw everything in my bag and headed out to my car. And froze when I remembered that Kyle was meeting me.

"Hey, what took so long? I was going to come in and make sure you hadn't drowned in the shower or something." She saw my face.

"What's wrong? Did something happen?" I took a breath and tried to act normally.

"Uh, yeah. One of the girls had to go to the hospital and she might have broken her wrist. So things were a little crazy." I took the green juice with a shaking hand that I hoped she didn't see. It was freezing, so we got in my car and I cranked the heat for her.

"Oh, I'm sorry. But you looked really freaked out." I was. Still. Sitting next to her wasn't helping. I realized I hadn't kissed her, so I leaned over and gave her a peck.

Shouldn't have done that.

"Okay, something is definitely wrong." I shook my head. She didn't let me get away with anything.

"I just had a talk with Midori. About us." She groaned.

"I had one with Grace too. She wanted to know a lot of details and got . . . really personal about things. She knows way too much about what lesbians do in bed, by the way and I really don't want to know how she knows all that." She shuddered and I wished I could laugh.

"Yeah, Midori didn't do that. She just . . . said some things." I knew I was digging myself into a hole, but I didn't know what else to do. Short of pushing her out of the car and driving away.

"Okay, babe, you're being really vague and it's freaking me out a little." She turned to face me and I scrambled to figure out what to say to her.

"It's nothing. It's nothing." I turned away from her, but she grabbed my face and made me look at her.

"Nope, I'm going to sit here and stare at you until you're uncomfortable enough to tell me. So there." I tried to get away, but she just held on.

"This is ridiculous," I said, but she just smiled.

"It's only ridiculous if it doesn't work."

"Kyle, please. I don't want to talk about it. Please." Her fingers stroked my cheeks.

"Oh, babe, what's got you so rattled? I want to help. Talk to me." Her voice pleaded and I wanted to tell her. But I couldn't. I just couldn't.

I closed my eyes and tried to pull away again, but she wouldn't let me.

"*Please.*" Her eyebrows drew together in concern, but she nodded.

"Okay," she said, but I could tell she was hurt.

"I'm sorry," I said, my voice cracking. Her thumbs brushed my skin.

"It's okay, babe. It's okay." She brought my face forward and kissed me. Even though I was being an asshole. Even though I was hiding something from her. She kissed me anyway.

Something major was up with Stella. I'd never seen her so freaked out. Completely freaked. She almost looked like she was going to be sick.

I wanted to know what it was, because I wanted to help her, but she closed right up and wouldn't tell. Just like she wouldn't tell me why she was such a bitch in front of everyone else, but not with me.

Stella had her secrets and I guess part of being with her was living with them. I could do it, because I wanted to be with her no matter what. It was a small price to pay for getting to kiss her and laugh with her and hold her hand.

She seemed like she wanted to be alone, so I left her and went home, feeling on edge. My parents asked what was wrong at dinner and I caved and told them. Not everything, but that Stella was being weird and I didn't know what to do about it.

"Do you think someone maybe said something mean to her?" Mom asked. That had been my first thought too. And my second thought was that someone had maybe threatened her. Who knows? But I was pretty sure she'd tell me about something like that. No, this was something different. And I was pretty sure Stella would have no problem telling someone that they could shove their homophobia right up their own ass.

"She just won't talk to me about certain things and it drives me crazy," I said, putting my head in my hands. I sighed and looked up to find my parents giving each other one of those looks that parents did when they didn't say anything out loud, but you could tell they were thinking the same thing. It was weird.

"Well, maybe you should give her some space? Some time? She might find that she'll want to come and talk to you, if you give her a little room." I'd thought about that and I didn't like it. I didn't like anything that put more space between us than there already was.

"I just don't want this to end before it's even started."

"Aw, honey, I'm sure it'll work out," Mom said. I loved that she was acting like this was just another relationship because, to her, it was.

"Girls are tough," Dad said and I burst out laughing.

"Doesn't make them any easier to understand being one, let me tell you," I said. In some ways I thought it was harder.

I texted Stella once that night, telling her I was thinking of her and if she wanted to talk, I was there. She sent a goodnight message back and thanked me, but that was it. I knew I was going to see her in English the next day and I had no idea what she was going to say or what I was going to say or what the hell to do.

I made the mistake of looking online and succeeded in confusing myself and making myself more anxious about the whole thing. I stopped before I worked myself into a frenzy and tried to sleep, but it didn't work.

My alarm rang after only a few fitful hours of sleep and I wanted to tell my mom that I was sick and stay in bed and have her skip work and fuss over me like I was a little girl again. But what if Stella decided she did want to talk and then I wasn't there? I couldn't risk it.

So I dragged my ass out of bed and got dressed and threw some concealer on under my eyes, grateful that my glasses distracted people from how bad my dark circles were.

I wanted to chew on my nails, but they were both still polished, which only made me think of Stella even more. To be fair, just about everything made me think of her.

She beat me to English and her head snapped up when I walked in. She looked gorgeous, as always, but I could tell she hadn't slept well either.

"Hey," I said, sliding into my seat next to her.

"Hey," she said, her voice rough.

"Are you okay? I was worried about you," I said under my breath. "I almost called you so many times." She looked straight ahead.

"I'm sorry."

I didn't want her to apologize. I wanted her to talk to me.

"It's okay," I said, feeling a horrible sinking feeling in the pit of my stomach. "I just wish you would trust me." That made her look at me.

"I do trust you," she said, as if I'd uttered something ridiculous.

"Then why won't you talk to me?" I hissed. Shit, girls were difficult. Worth it, but difficult.

She looked like she was going to respond, but then didn't.

"I'm sorry," she said again, and I could tell she meant it. There was something holding her back. Someone must have broken her trust. Really broken it. There was so much more to Stella than met the eye and I was determined to find out. I wasn't going down without a hell of a fight. If she wanted one, she had one on her hands. I was stubborn as hell.

She had to work at the vet clinic on Wednesday night, so I drove there and waited for her to come out. I didn't think this would qualify as stalking. If she told me to leave, I'd get in my car, but I was going to give this a shot. I had to.

She didn't look surprised to see me when she came out, dressed in scrubs with her hair up. I'd never seen her in her work clothes and what looked like crap on most people on her, of course, were painfully cute.

"Just tell me to go, and I'll go," I said, holding my hands up to stop her from having the first word. She pulled her keys out of her purse, and when she exhaled her breath clouded in the air.

"I don't want you to," she said, and I knew she was really struggling.

"You don't have to talk to me. I don't want to put you in crisis. I don't want to tear you apart. I just want you to be happy." She started to cry and I pulled her into my arms, letting her rest her head on my shoulder. We were both freezing and she started to shake, but I wasn't moving. I would freeze to death out here. I would let all my fingers and toes turn black and fall off from frostbite. I would stay here and hold my girl.

I had come to the realization that I liked Stella. A lot. A lot, a lot. I wasn't going to call it "serious" yet, but it was getting there. This girl was probably going to wreck me and I was going to stand there and let her.

She finally lifted her head and sniffed. She had snot coming from her nose, but it was a testament to her beauty that she still took my breath away. I pulled her toward my car and made her get in, fishing a tissue out from the center console and handing it to her. She dabbed at her nose and her eyes and then stared out the windshield.

"You only know me now. You know me as the ice-cold bitch. I wasn't always like that and I think you know that. But I never told you why." I waited, nearly holding my breath.

"I wasn't popular in school. At all. I was more into books and my mom ran off and I don't really know why people didn't want to be friends with me. I tried. I tried so hard and in third grade, a group of girls that I wanted to be friends with started asking me to hang out with them. I was so excited that they invited me to their parties and sleepovers, but they only invited me to torment me. And it wasn't just stuff they said, there were other things they did." She shuddered.

"Anyway, I was so desperate to be friends with them, that I took it. I let them treat me worse than garbage. For years. There wasn't a day that went by that they didn't do something awful. As we got older, they got better at hiding what they were doing, so teachers didn't notice. I never told anyone. I had myself convinced that if I only put up with it long enough, they would let me in. They would like me." She inhaled and closed her eyes for a minute. I reached out tentatively and took her hand. She let me.

"I don't want to talk about the details, because honestly? I think I blocked a lot of it out. I didn't tell my dad. I wanted to handle it myself. Gabe knew, but there wasn't much he could do to protect me. So when I finally got to high school, I decided that I wasn't going to let that happen again. I wasn't going to be a victim. I was going to be a stone-cold bitch and not let them see that they could hurt me." Everything completely clicked into place. I knew she had a good reason and that was definitely it.

"That makes sense," I said and she looked back at me.

"Really? It doesn't make me a terrible person?" I frowned.

"Why would it make you a terrible person to protect yourself from people who hurt you for years?" She looked down at our hands.

"I don't know. I've never told anyone this. Midori already knew because she moved here in seventh grade. But other than that, no one else knows." I was honored. And totally pissed off. I wanted to throttle those stupid girls. WTF was wrong with them?

"I want to throat punch them all," I said and she laughed, just a little.

"I would like to see that," she said. "Anyway, things are different now and I guess I just got so used to it that I don't really know how to stop. And I was scared that if I let people see who I really was, that they wouldn't like it." Now that was ridiculous. Her personality was awesome. She was funny and sweet and so, so smart.

"Everyone would love you." There was a voice that whispered in the back of my mind *you already do*.

"I think that's an overstatement and you're a little biased, but thanks. That's really nice, Ky." I put my arms out and she let me hug her.

"Thank you so much for trusting me. I know this is a big deal for you. I just want to live up to it." She kissed my cheek.

"I do trust you. I don't know if I've ever trusted someone like I trust you. I mean, my family yes, but this is different. And then there are ways I don't trust you." The bottom dropped out of my stomach.

"What do you mean?"

She stared into my eyes, unblinking.

"I'm afraid that you're going to break my heart."

I couldn't breathe for several seconds.

"Well, that makes two of us," I said and we just gazed at one another.

"So, this is happening," she said and I nodded.

"This is happening."

Neither of us could say it. Not yet.

"Will you be my girlfriend?" I blurted out to stop myself from saying something else.

"Yeah. Yeah, I will." It felt like a proposal. I almost wished I had a ring. A visual reminder that we were together.

"This is a very intense moment," I said, stating the obvious. Stella just closed her eyes and brought her face to mine.

"Shut up."

"Shut up, *girlfriend*," I said into her mouth.

"Shut up, girlfriend."

CHAPTER 16

Stella

I couldn't believe that I told her, but just one day of essentially ignoring her was too much. I had been so miserable at work that even a basket of kittens couldn't cheer me up. It wasn't that I couldn't live without her, it was that I didn't like the way I'd treated her. I didn't like the words I'd said and I couldn't let it end like that. I would hate myself forever.

Even before she showed up, I vowed that I was going to call her and ask her to meet me somewhere so we could talk. But, of course, she beat me to it.

And then we'd talked and I'd told her and it was okay. Better than okay. I told her that I more than liked her and she felt the same and now I had a girlfriend.

My very first girlfriend.

We both had tons of homework that couldn't be ignored, so we couldn't hang out for long, so making out in the backseat of her car had to be cut tragically short.

I'd managed to get my hand most of the way up her shirt, brushing the underside of her bra. So. Close.

"We should stop," she gasped, breaking our kiss. I nodded, and ran a shaky hand through my hair.

"Uh huh," I said, pushing myself up with my arms. We'd gotten horizontal and if we'd had more time, we probably would have gotten a lot more naked.

My brain was scrambled and I was so turned on that I was in pain. I needed a shower. Stat.

We both scrambled out of her car and we were a little shaky, trying to get ourselves together to actually drive.

Kyle kissed me goodbye and whispered in my ear.

"I'm going to think about you all night." I shivered and she gave me a sly smile and wave before she yelled "Bye, girlfriend!" and drove away.

"Well, shit," I said, leaning against my car and telling my heart to calm down.

——————◖◆◗——————

"You stayed late tonight," Dad said when I walked through the door and into the living room. I bet my face was still a little red, even though I'd driven past the house twice to try and get myself looking normal so I could face him. I sat on the couch nearest his leather wing chair where he read for pleasure.

"Um, sort of? I stayed late, but not to work. I, ah, had a talk with Kyle. You remember meeting her, right?" He put down his book.

"How could I forget?" A hint of a smile started to emerge.

"Stop it," I said, blushing.

"She's very cute. And smart, I'm guessing, if she's in AP English." I nodded.

"She is. She's number four in our class."

"Very nice. Is there something you want to tell me about her?" Not really, but if I wanted to have her over, I was going to have to do this.

"Kyle and I are kind of . . . together. Together, together." He laughed.

"I get the point, Star. She's your girlfriend. Is that the term teens still use?" I raised one eyebrow. What else would you call it?

"Um, yes? A new term hasn't been invented yet, so we're going with girlfriend for now." Saying the word out loud made me want to do a bunch of standing back tucks.

"That's a big step. But she seems like a very nice girl. I'd like to meet her, talk to her more, if you want to have her over." My dad had never been one of those overbearing types that would threaten anyone that Gabe or I dated.

"Yeah, she's forcing me to meet her parents, so it's only fair, I guess." He chuckled.

"Seems so." We lapsed into silence and then I couldn't deal with it.

"I really like her. A lot." He gave me a gentle smile.

"You seem giddy. I haven't seen you like that." Because I never had been. I'd never felt so many overwhelming and fluttery and confusing and wonderful things all at once.

"The timing sucks. Because it's going to end. We're both going to head to different colleges and maybe try and stick it out for a while, but then we'll stop calling and it will just end." Dad leaned back in his chair. He always did that when he was going to give me some advice. He was very good at it.

"Or maybe it won't. Usually going into something thinking that you're going to lose is an excellent way to ensure that you do." I knew that, but could it really work? How many people actually stayed with their high school sweethearts? I'd heard the statistics and they were low. I bet they didn't even have any on LGBT couples in those kinds of surveys. Because we didn't really exist, probably.

"I don't know. I hate thinking about it. I just want to think about now and then deal with that later."

"That's probably a good idea. But give it a chance before you write it off completely. Love doesn't work out for everyone, I should know, but it can for some people. You might just get to be one of them." It was a little pessimistic, but Dad was like that. He didn't sugarcoat reality. Never had.

"Yeah, I guess. Anyway." I got up and gave him a kiss on the forehead. He wrapped his arm around my waist.

"I'm so proud of the woman you're becoming, my Star. So proud to call you my daughter." I had tears in my eyes that I wiped away before I hugged him back and went to the kitchen to make some dinner.

"**Y**ou're totally my girlfriend," Kyle said later that night as we sat in our separate beds in our separate rooms, pretending that we were together.

"Yup. You talked me into it. I was powerless against you," I said, being dramatic.

"Oh, shut up. I'm not the hot one." I snorted.

"I beg to differ, but we're never going to agree on that one."

"Probably not."

I leaned back and twirled some hair around my finger.

"Are we going to be out now? At school and everything?" I asked.

"Can we wait until next week?" she said.

"Absolutely. And I think we should prepare ourselves for people being . . . less than welcoming. Our families and besties are one thing, but who knows. That's another reason I didn't want to come out until I was in college. I figured it would just give everyone ammunition to shoot at me again. But now it doesn't seem so bad. I mean, I haven't dealt with it yet, so I might totally regret this." I laughed.

"Yeah, I've thought about that a lot. I mean, I don't care what people think, but having someone say something horrible about you in front of me is something that would make me so angry, I can feel my blood boiling just thinking about it. Ugh, I don't even want to talk about it." I could hear the anger in her voice and I felt the same way. I had protected myself, but I would slay some fucking dragons for Kyle.

"We aren't the first couple at school, though. There's Jane and Lexi and then Polly and Tris. I know there are more. They all hang out in a group together." It was a small school, but I'd always consciously avoided even making eye contact with any of them. Afraid that they would know. Afraid that they could see me. With their gaydar.

"That's true. Do you think we should make friends with them? It might be nice to talk to someone else who's been through this. Other than us." I'd thought about that too. As much as I loved the girls on the cheer team and Midori, this was something I couldn't share with them. They could sympathize, but they didn't know what it was like to care about another girl like this.

"But how do we go about it? Just walk up to them and ask to join their group?" That sounded painfully awkward. Definitely didn't want to do that.

"I don't know. Let's get through this week and tackle that next week. I feel like we have to go about this in steps. We'll get there eventually. I honestly can't wait for the day when I can just walk down the hallway with you and not worry." Yeah, me too.

"And when we can go on real dates not in one of our living rooms. I want to show you off, you sexy nerd." That made her laugh.

"I wanna show you off too, you beautiful thing. People are probably going to think I've lost my mind for going out with you. After they get over the initial shock that Kyle Blake and Stella Lewis are gay as fuck." I burst out laughing and couldn't stop.

"I'm kind of looking forward to the looks on people's faces," she said. I hadn't thought of it that way. I'd always thought about it in a negative way. But maybe it would be good. It had been so far.

"You have a bad case of the giggles tonight, baby," she said because I couldn't stop laughing. "I think it's time to go to bed."

I stopped laughing and took a deep breath.

"Okay, I guess. I'll see you tomorrow. Bye, Ky."

I sent her a text the minute I woke up with a picture of me doing a kissy face.

Good morning, my girlfriend.

She sent one back of her blowing me a kiss.

Hey, girlfriend, hey.

I skipped to the bathroom and I couldn't stop smiling. I also couldn't wait to get to school, which was pretty unusual. I didn't hate school, but if I had a choice, I wouldn't go there every day. I'd much rather hang out in a huge library somewhere, reading whatever I wanted, day after day. Someday I'd get to do that. Maybe.

I just happened to see Kyle getting out of her car when I parked in the student lot and I honked at her. She turned around to glare at the asshole who'd honked and then her face lit up when she saw me.

That look. That look was everything. I wanted to see that look on that face every day. Forever.

I told myself to chill out, but it was hard when I got out of the car and Kyle came over to say hello. The lot was busy and people were calling out greetings to one another and talking, so we had an audience so we couldn't kiss or anything.

"I couldn't wait to see you, is that crazy?" she asked as we stood with several feet of space between us, both leaning on my car.

I looked up at the grey sky. They were calling for snow, which was bizarre since it wasn't even November yet. It would definitely mess with the football schedule.

"No, because I couldn't wait to see you," I said, turning back toward her.

"I want to kiss you so bad right now, baby," she said, reaching out to touch my face, but then pulling back.

"Soon. Soon you can do that all you want. It's Wednesday. Just a few more days and the week is over. And next week . . ." I trailed off.

Next week.

"We'll have to make a plan." She agreed.

"Definitely. I think that means we should spend the entire weekend together making said plan. We really have to think through all the possible scenarios." She was saying one thing, but meaning something entirely different, something that made my skin tingle.

"I think that can be arranged," I said, my fingers aching to touch her.

"Good. It's a date." She winked and then pushed off my car to walk to homeroom. I gave her a head start and then walked behind her. Mostly to check out her ass. She'd started wearing tighter jeans lately for some reason and I was very much enjoying the view.

I had to go to a different building and by the time I sat down in homeroom, I had a text on my phone.

Stop ogling my ass.

I snorted and then sent her back a winky face.

"So? What's the update?" Grace said to me as we were supposed to be doing an experiment in chem.

"With what?" I asked, adjusting the height of the flame so it didn't hit the ceiling and burn a hole through it.

"With you-know-who?" I stood up.

"Voldemort?" Grace gave me a look like I was being dense.

"Oh, oh, *that*. Things are good? Really good." I bit my lip and Grace bumped her hip with mine.

"Sounds like it. So are you guys going public?" I did a quick sweep of the room, but everyone else was immersed in what they were doing.

"Soon," I said and then we both pretended to be working very diligently as our teacher walked by.

"I've got your back. And hers, by extension. And I think I should get to hang out with both of you. I've never seen you in a relationship like this before." That was because there hadn't been one. There was nothing like this. I didn't know if it was because we were both girls. I'd never find out. But I did know that what I felt for Stella was something big.

Something beautiful and new and amazing.

"You get all smiley when you're thinking about her."

"Stop it," I said, smacking her arm.

———————◆———————

"**I** feel like we haven't seen you in forever," Paige said at lunch. I had no idea what she was talking about. I'd eaten with them yesterday.

"Okay?" I said, unsure of whether or not I was supposed to apologize.

"You've just seemed kinda distant," Molly chimed in. I looked around and every single one of them was wearing an uncomfortable look.

"Is this some sort of intervention?" I said, looking around and landing on Grace. She had her arms crossed and looked like she didn't approve of whatever they were doing.

"No, that's stupid. We just miss you, that's all." Molly's face went red and I had half a mind to get up from the damn table and leave all of them.

"I'm literally sitting right here. Talking to you. I'm not off slitting my wrists, or hanging out and smoking pot under the overpass. So I really have no idea what the fuck is going on." I didn't mean to get so pissed, but I felt like I was being attacked or something.

"Just leave her alone, guys. All of you," Grace said, sending a glare around that made some of them cower. The guys had been avoiding eye contact with me the whole time.

"So, did anyone hear what Chad Hoskins got arrested with?" Grace said and that got everyone talking again. Thanks, Chad.

But I still had an uneasy feeling in my stomach when I tossed my tray.

"I told them not to," Grace said in my ear. "I really did. I told them to leave you alone and that you were fine, but then Molly started going on and on about her cousin who's on crack or something and it got blown out of proportion. If you decide to, ah, *tell people*, next week, I think they'll lay off. Not that that's a reason to do it. But it would give them an explanation. You know?"

I understood what she was saying, but I still felt like they were backing me into a corner.

Fuck it. If they were going to be assholes about me being happy, then they weren't my real friends anyway. And since when did happy = being on drugs?

Fucked up. I sent Stella a text about it.

OMG, your friends are weird. But maybe they'll leave you alone next week?

Hopefully. We didn't have anyone else gay in our group that I knew of. No one really said anything outright that was homophobic, but you never knew. It was like rolling dice, but instead of winning money, you got the freedom to live and not be harassed.

"So I talked to one of the other gays today," Stella said that afternoon as we hung out at her house. Her dad was teaching late tonight, so we had several hours of uninterrupted time. I wanted to spend most of it making out and doing other things, but she seemed to want to talk.

"Which one?" I asked.

"Tris. It just kind of happened. She was in the bathroom and we were using the sinks at the same time. I said hello and she gave me a look like I was going to punch her in the face. So then I tried a smile and she sort of gave me one back and then scurried away." I couldn't stop laughing. My girl was intimidating.

"You probably scared the shit out of her. I bet she thinks you're going to target her or something. It's going to be funny to see what she says when she knows the truth." She laughed with me and then moved so her head was in my lap. I ran my fingers through her hair and she closed her eyes.

"That feels really good. I can't remember the last time someone else played with my hair." She curled up almost like a cat. I wouldn't have been surprised if she started purring.

"Don't fall asleep, baby." We had some stupid reality show on that neither of us was paying attention to. I was too busy focusing all my attention on her.

"I won't. What if they hate us?"

"Who?" She turned her head and looked up at me.

"The other gays." Was she serious?

"Why would they? And don't they kind of have to accept us? Based on the fact that there's safety in numbers." I had no experience with this, but it made sense. And we had a lot in common with them, so why wouldn't we get along?

I had definitely realized, early on in knowing her, that Stella had issues when it came to trusting other people. Especially trusting that they weren't going to hate her right off the bat. It was shitty, but the only way she'd realize that not everyone was an asshole was to introduce her to more people who were going to adore her just the way she was. Not the bitch queen. The beautiful girl who spent an entire summer with Tolstoy. The girl who loved animals and laughed in the library and was passionate about cheerleading. If anyone didn't like that girl, they had some serious issues.

"I guess you're right. I just don't like meeting new people." I stroked her temple.

"I know, baby. But I think this will be good. For both of us. As much as I like living in our bubble, I think it's time for us to get out. I don't want to turn into people that never leave their houses or go out in the sunlight." She giggled.

"I think we're going to be fine." I leaned down and kissed her head.

"Yeah, we are. We're gonna be fine."

The weather warmed up again (if you don't like the weather in Maine, wait five minutes) so the game was on for Friday. I was a little nervous about going, but excited about seeing Stella cheer. She was just so good at it.

My friends had backed off after that little "talk" they'd had with me during lunch on Wednesday, but I could tell they were still watching me.

"Don't let them force you into anything," Grace said, leaning over as we froze our asses off on the bleachers.

"I'm not. Stella and I are tired of hiding. We want to be like everyone else. And it's not like we're ashamed, you know? I'm proud of her." My eyes flicked over to her as she made a funny face at Midori.

"Good. And if you need anyone to kick someone's ass for you, I volunteer." I didn't want her to do that, but her heart was in the right place.

"Thanks."

"What are best friends for?" She put her arm around me and we snuggled closer together.

"I wish someone looked at me like that," she said and I tore my eyes away from Stella. Again.

"Huh?"

Grace nodded in Stella's direction.

"I wish someone looked at me the way you look at her." I gaped at her and she just grinned.

"It's really sweet. I'm not jealous, I swear." Last year, Grace had broken up with her boyfriend she'd had since junior high when he went to a private school an hour away. I knew she still cried about it every now and then. I almost felt like I was rubbing my happiness in her face.

"Grace—" I started to say, but she put her hand up.

"It's not your fault. I'm really, really happy for you. Just makes me miss when I felt like that." I put my arm around her.

"You will again."

"Promise?"

"Promise."

The game finally started, but I paid even less attention to what was happening on the field than I usually did. Too busy looking at my girl.

She kept flashing looks back at me and once she even winked. She'd asked me if I wanted to come hang out with her and her friends after the game and I'd turned her down, but now I was rethinking it.

"Do you want to go to the barn party with me?" There was a guy, Raylan Ford, whose parents had a farm with an old barn on their property and didn't really care what he and his friends did to it since they were just going to demolish it anyway.

Grace made a face.

"I'd rather not subject myself to the rednecks tonight." I had a feeling she'd say that, and I didn't blame her. As liberal as our little town was, it was still incredibly white and people didn't get called out on their shit as much as they should sometimes.

"Yeah, okay," I said, looking back at Stella.

"But for you, I'll do it. Unless someone says something. Then I'm out." I stared at her.

"Seriously?" That was a best friend right there.

"Yeah, who knows? It could be fun." I wasn't sure about that. I'd never gone to one of the barn parties because it had never appealed to me, but Stella appealed to me and anywhere she was, that was where I wanted to be. So we were going to a barn party.

———————————◆◆———————————

I waited on the bleachers for Stella to pack up her stuff and for most of the crowd from the game to disperse. Grace said she had to "get something from her car" so she'd left me by myself a few minutes ago.

"Hey, baby," Stella said, coming over. "I bet I could give you a hug right now and no one would think anything." I got up and put my arms out and she walked into them.

"Hi," I said, hugging her and not even caring that she was sweaty.

"Hi back. I saw you staring at me."

"Am I not allowed to stare at my girlfriend?" She pulled back and I reached up to adjust the bow she had on top of her head, adorning her high ponytail.

"Oh, that's right. You totally are." She gave me a sweet smile.

"So, I think Grace and I are going to the barn party." Her face lit up.

"Really? That would be so great. Then we can all hang out together. My theory is if we bring our groups together enough, they'll just mesh and make one big group." She was so cute.

"We'll see." I gave her another hug and said I would meet her at the party with Grace.

I headed to my car and found Grace leaning on it, messing with her phone.

"I can drive so we only have to take one car. You just say the word and I'll bring you back."

She gave me a thumbs up and we got in the car.

CHAPTER 17

Stella

I was both apprehensive and exited that Kyle was coming to the party. Both feelings churned in my stomach as I drove myself and Midori way out to the boonies where the barn was.

"So she's coming?" I'd told Midori that Kyle and Grace were going to meet us there.

"Yup. We're not going to be official, but this is the first time we've hung out in public together, so . . ." I turned off onto a dirt road and slowed down so my car wouldn't bottom out on the potholes.

"It's a shame you can't just be together like everyone else." I swerved to avoid a huge branch and winced as we bumped over the uneven road. We'd had to take the back way to the farm because the cops in town liked to cruise and try and find parties to bust.

"Yeah, it is. Someday, though."

At last we arrived and I parked my car in the field next to a rusted-out truck and looked for Kyle. I sent her a text and then saw her waving from another row of cars.

Midori and I walked over and joined Kyle and Grace.

"Hey," I said to both of them. I hoped this wasn't going to be painfully awkward.

Kyle just grabbed my hand and then gave me a kiss on the cheek. I was stunned when I pulled back.

"Sorry, couldn't help it."

"They're so cute it's painful," Grace said to Midori.

"Tell me about it."

And that was it.

The four of us headed to the party, Kyle and I holding hands since it was dark and no one would probably see. Grace and Midori started talking about comics (apparently Midori's older sister was going to college to do the art for graphic novels) and completely ignored us.

"Well, that worked out," Kyle said in my ear as we approached the barn. A couple of people had a bonfire going near (but not too near) the barn and were throwing shit on it and yelling as the sparks flared up. There was music coming from the open barn doors.

I sighed and dropped Kyle's hand. It was like a punch in the stomach until she grabbed it back.

"No. I'm not hiding. I'm not stopping myself from touching you because of other people. Seriously, fuck that." I stopped walking and turned to face her.

"Really?"

"Hell, yeah. I was thinking about it all day today and I'm ready. I'm ready for this." She held up our joined hands and I felt tears in the corners of my eyes.

"So this is it? We're doing this at a shitty barn party where everyone will probably be too stoned or drunk to remember on Monday?" She shrugged.

"Guess so."

Midori and Grace had stopped walking ahead of us, just at the entrance to the barn. They both looked down at our hands and then started clapping.

"Oh, shut up," Kyle said.

"I used to think you were a complete bitch, but Kyle has assured me that you aren't, so I'm giving you the benefit of the doubt," Grace said, looking at me.

"Thank you?"

"Uh huh," she said and then started talking to Midori again.

"Let's go, baby," Kyle said, tugging on my hand.

<hr />

I wasn't sure what I expected when we walked in. Maybe an explosion. Or for everyone to comically freeze and gasp in unison.

Neither of those things happened.

"We got this," Kyle said, squeezing my hand. A few people glanced over, looked down at our joined hands and then just started talking again. One dude yelled out "Hey, dykes!" but he was standing on a barrel and fell off immediately after.

"This isn't so bad," I said as we found a corner away from the music that had a few rotting benches we could sit on. We had to walk through pockets of pot smoke and I was glad the ceiling of the barn was basically gone so we weren't drowning in it. The beams were strung with lanterns and half-dead twinkle lights, all powered with orange extension cords. The entire thing was probably a fire hazard, but so far, so good.

"We're going to get drinks," Midori said. "Do you guys want anything?" I looked at Kyle.

"Water? Or Coke. Nothing alcoholic," I said and Kyle agreed. Grace and Midori went off for the drinks and it was just the two of us.

"This is so weird," Kyle said, leaning closer to me and then kissing me on the cheek.

"But not weird at the same time," I said, kissing the back of her hand.

"Exactly."

A few girls from the squad came over and they were stunned for a few seconds, but after we talked to them and said, yes, we were together, they wanted to know everything.

"OMG, can I come to your wedding?" Candace asked.

"Um, we literally just started dating. I think it's a little early for that. Right, babe?" Kyle blushed and there was a chorus of awwws. It was a bit like being an exhibit in a zoo. Finally, their curiosity was satisfied and a bunch of them went to dance.

"I guess we're cute," Kyle said as Midori and Grace came back and handed us our drinks.

"You are cute. It's gross," Grace said, popping the top of her soda. A lot of the cheer girls were dancing with their boyfriends or other guys all in one big heaving clump. I remembered doing that and it had been fun, but I wasn't a fan of having a guy pressing his dick into my ass and then getting a hard-on while we were grinding.

"Whatever," Kyle said.

I expected more attention from the guys, but a lot of them were out at the bonfire, busy with their own girls, or drunk off their asses.

I did hear a few wolf whistles and one guy walked by and asked if we would bang him, but we just ignored him. It honestly wasn't that bad. So far. I kept waiting for the other shoe to drop.

"I shouldn't stay too late. My parents are actually enforcing my curfew now," Kyle said with a rueful smile. "I never had a reason to stay out before you, girlfriend."

"I'm flattered," I said, fluttering my lashes at her.

"Hey, you're not the only gays at this party," Grace said, pointing with her soda can.

Across the room were Tris and her girlfriend, Polly, standing close together and talking with some people. I'd never seen them interacting that much outside of their usual group.

"Should we go say something?" Kyle asked. "What's the protocol here?"

I laughed.

"I have no idea. But maybe we should let them come to us. I'm sure word has gotten out by now." It definitely would by Monday. We'd really done this with a bang, but why the hell not?

Someone turned the music up since more people had moved out to the makeshift dance floor in the middle of the room.

"Do you want to dance with me?" I asked Kyle and her face went white.

"Um, no. I don't think so." She looked away from me. I glanced at Grace and she just gave me a shrug.

"Why not?" I asked, brushing a wisp of hair over her ear.

She heaved a heavy sigh.

"In case you hadn't noticed, I'm not very coordinated. And you are a goddess." I almost laughed. No one had ever called me that before.

"Everyone can dance." She gave me a look as if I'd said something stupid.

"Oh, this is ridiculous, come on." I stood up and pulled her to her feet, against her protests.

"We won't go over there," I said, pointing to the main floor. "We'll dance right here."

I closed my eyes for a second and the song switched to a country song with a fast and driving beat.

"Stellll," Kyle whined. "I don't want to do this." I gave her the quickest of kisses and winked.

"You will."

I turned around and grabbed her hands, placing them on my hips as I found the beat of the music and started moving my hips. Kyle was stiff for a second.

"Just follow me," I said, leaning my head back against her.

She finally started moving with me.

"Fuck," she breathed in my ear. I smiled and melted into her.

Our bodies fit. Perfectly. As if they were made for one another. Curves against curves. Her fingers dug into my hips and I couldn't get over the feel of her against my back and her hips moving with mine.

The only downside was that I couldn't see her face, so I rotated until we were facing one another.

She didn't let go of my hips. I put my hands on her shoulders and then we were dancing face-to-face and I would never, for the rest of my life, forget the way she looked at me.

As if she wanted to devour me and worship me at the same time. I couldn't look away from her green eyes.

I'd never wanted anything the way I wanted her.

The song finally ended and we were both breathing hard. It flipped to another country song that I wasn't as fond of.

"I want you so bad right now," Kyle said, pressing her forehead to mine. My fingers shook a little as I held her face and kissed her lips.

"Me, too."

Our eyes locked and I knew it was only a matter of time. I wanted to take her hand and drag her out and fuck her in the backseat of my car. Hell, I'd settle for a nice patch of grass.

"I can't even think," Kyle said. "I can't even think about anything but you."

The words clogged the back of my throat, desperate to get out. I clamped my mouth shut. I couldn't. Not yet.

Not yet.

"I want to do so many things right now, Ky," I whispered. She made a little sound in the back of her throat that didn't help the situation at all.

"I think I have an idea what you're thinking of."

I smiled.

"Oh, do you?"

"Would you like me to draw you a diagram?" I laughed and then someone cleared their throat. I turned away from Kyle to snarl at whoever had interrupted us, only to find Tris and Polly standing there with amused looks on their faces.

"Can we help you?" I asked, trying to be nice.

"We, ah, just wanted to say hello," Tris said. She and Polly made a cute pair, with Tris rocking a button-up and suspenders, and Polly in a dress that would have made a 50s housewife proud, and bright lipstick. Tonight it was an almost neon pink.

"And you had to do that *now?*" I wondered aloud. Kyle stepped away from me.

"Sorry about her. She's just a little cranky." I gaped at her.

"I know what that's like," Polly said, shooting a look at Tris, who was busy staring at me with her eyes narrowed.

"Don't be grumpy. However cute it is," Polly said to Tris, leaning up on her tiptoes to kiss Tris' cheek. Polly was significantly shorter than Tris, even with her heels on.

"So, looks like you two are . . ." Polly said, trailing off, letting us fill in the blanks.

Kyle rested her chin on my shoulder and slid her arms around me.

"Yup," she said. "Surprised?"

Polly and Tris shared a look.

"A little," Polly admitted. "But you never know, do you? How long have you guys been together?"

"Little while," I said. Tris was still giving me a look like I was just fucking with her.

"We're not faking it. If that's what you're thinking," I said directly to Tris.

"I wasn't thinking anything," she said.

"Yeah, okay. The way you've been looking at us is totally normal, sure." Kyle squeezed my sides to tell me to shut up.

"Just surprised. Didn't expect you to be one of us." That made me want to start chanting "One of us, one of us."

I raised an eyebrow.

"So being gay is like a cult now?" Tris rolled her eyes.

"You know that's not what I meant."

"Okay, then. I'm gay, so is she, and we're super gay together. Got it? Good." I turned around and kissed Kyle full on the mouth. I didn't need to prove anything to them, but I did it anyway.

"Does that clear it up for you?" I asked, turning back around, feeling a little dizzy. Kyle's mouth always did that to me.

"You're really cute together," Polly said, leaning against Tris. "You're like the perfect femme couple." At least she hadn't called us lipstick lesbians.

I leaned back against Kyle again.

"Thank you," I said.

"So, now that we've established that we're all girls who like girls, maybe we could, um, talk like normal people?" Kyle said. "Because it's just been the two of us and it would be really nice to talk to someone else."

That seemed to do the trick.

Tris finally melted and we started talking about our various coming out stories. Guess Tris' family wasn't as accepting as mine and Kyle's and she'd had a real hard time of it.

"I'm sorry," I said, really meaning it. She shrugged it off.

"Not your fault. Just the way things are. That's why I can't wait to get out of this hick town and go to college."

"Where are you headed?"

"Austin," she said, putting her arm over Polly's shoulder. "We're both going to UT." I still hadn't figured out where the hell I wanted to go. Kyle and I had been purposely avoiding college talk. I didn't want to be one of those people who had to factor in their girlfriend for their college decision. Even though I probably would.

"Yup, it's gonna be awesome. We're going to get a little apartment and a dog and it will be sunny all the time," Polly said. She was bright and bubbly and constantly moving. I liked her. The jury was still out on Tris, but she seemed to be warming up. I wasn't really one to talk about being standoffish anyway.

Grace and Midori came over and we introduced them.

Somehow, we all ended up talking for a while and it wasn't a big deal at all.

Kyle squeezed my shoulder.

"Baby, I've got to get home." I turned and gave her a sad smile.

"Okay, I'll go with you to your car." Grace wanted to stay and asked if I could give her a ride.

"See you on Monday!" Polly said, waving at us as we left. I took Kyle's hand as we slowly made our way back to her car. The bonfire had mostly burned itself out, but there were still people throwing shit on it to get it going again.

"That was interesting," Kyle said.

"Just a little bit. What do you think Monday is going to be like?" She shook her head.

"No idea. But if it was anything like this, I think it'll be good. I guess people just don't care. Which is awesome for us." Definitely. I knew it wasn't all going to be good, but so far, my worst fears hadn't come true.

"I loved dancing with you," she said when we got to her car.

"Yeah?" I asked and then had the breath knocked out of me as she pushed me up against the door of the car.

"Yeah," she said before her mouth crashed down on mine and she kissed me like she needed me to breathe.

Her hands fumbled under my shirt and then she was caressing my bare skin and I was honestly going to die or shatter into a million pieces. She didn't get to be the only one doing the touching, so I slid my fingers under the hem of her shirt and brushed the smooth skin of her stomach.

We both trembled and gasped and it was going to kill me.

"I want you so much," she said into my mouth.

"You can have me. You can have everything," I said back.

She laughed. A low, sexy sound.

"Is that so?" Her fingers brushed the edge of my bra and I wished I wasn't wearing one.

"Yes. Fuck, yes."

She pulled back to look into my eyes.

"*Everything?*"

I knew exactly what she was asking, and what my answer would mean for both of us.

"Yes."

I didn't really mean to attack her like that, it just kind of happened. There were no protests as I kissed her and shoved my hands up her shirt. I'd been wanting to touch her skin since we'd danced.

Holy shit, the dancing. I hadn't known it was going to be like *that*. I'd pictured tripping over my feet and embarrassing myself, but she'd taken the lead and it turned out that moving my hips with hers didn't require any thinking on my part.

My body just wanted hers. Followed hers. It was natural, to be with her like that. It had made me want to tell her to drive somewhere and park, but then we'd been interrupted. I definitely had to go home now, but I wasn't going to stop thinking about it.

I also wasn't going to stop thinking about telling Stella how I felt about her. *Really* tell her. Because there was only one word for it and I wanted to tell her before we had sex. I wanted her to know that it wasn't just about needing to fuck her.

"Me too," I said. "I want you to have everything. I want it to be you." *I always want it to be you.*

She smiled slowly.

"I will keep that in mind. Later. When I'm in bed." I groaned and she giggled.

"You're just as bad, you know. My wrists have been getting quite a workout since I fell in love with you."

"What?"

She gasped, as if she hadn't meant to say it.

"Oh, shit. I said that out loud, didn't I?" I grabbed onto her shoulders because I felt like I was going to fall over.

"Did you just say that you love me?" My voice squeaked on the word. She swallowed and I could see the panic in her eyes.

"Yes. I did. Because I do. Love you. I don't care if it's too soon, or of we're seniors and heading to different colleges. I don't care. I love you, baby." She stroked my face and I wondered if it was possible for your heart to stop and still live.

"You love me?" There were tears in her eyes.

"Yeah, I do. I tried to fight it, but you're just too damn cute." I laughed a little, still completely overwhelmed.

"Okay. You love me. That's really good, I guess, because I love you too. It would be bad if one of us felt it and the other one didn't. But we're good." She squealed and threw herself on me.

"I thought it was going to freak you out, which is why I hadn't said it before." I leaned into her, smelling her hair.

"I've wanted to say it too. Guess we're both idiots." We laughed together and I reluctantly let her go.

"I really, really have to get home or else my parents are going to kill me. And I don't want them getting mad at me because then they won't let you come over or let me come see you, so." I babbled. Stella gave me one last lingering kiss.

"Okay. I'll see you tomorrow, then." We had plans to hang out all day together, including going to the movies and having lunch. Like a real couple.

"See you tomorrow, baby." I didn't want to let her go.

"Oh, by the way, I love you," she said.

"Oh, hey, me too," I said, getting into my car.

She loved me.

I made it home with two minutes to spare.

"Did you have fun with Grace?" Mom asked. She looked up from the paperback she was reading. When I'd texted her to say that I was going out after the game, I told her Grace and I were getting pizza with the rest of my friends. Oops.

"Yeah, we did actually." I didn't want to walk too close to her because I was pretty sure my clothes reeked of pot smoke. The one downside of the night.

"Good, good. Listen, I want to talk with you." Uh oh. I leaned against the wall, but she patted the spot next to her on the couch.

I reluctantly walked over because saying no would only make her more suspicious.

"I know you're going out with Stella now and you know your father and I fully support it, but I don't want you to take that to mean we don't have rules for you. If you were dating a boy, we'd have the same rules." Actually, I'd been wondering when she was going to throw this at me. Stella couldn't get me pregnant, but that wasn't their only concern, I was sure.

"Okay," I said. She stared at me, probably expecting more resistance.

"Okay, so. Your curfew is still in place and when you go out on dates, we want to know where you're going and when you're going to be back. I would also prefer that you seriously consider the consequences of any, ah, activity." Shit, we were having a sex talk. We'd had one before, but now things were different.

"I'm not going to tell you what to do because I know you're smart enough to know what's right for you, but I do want you to be careful.

Okay? And I know you're going to be off at college and can do whatever you want, but I'm still having a problem realizing that you're all grown up. When did that happen?" She sighed.

"Thanks. I can do that," I said.

"Good. I can see how much you care about her, and I just want to wrap you up in a bubble so you don't get your heart broken, but I know that I can't do that."

"I really like her, Mom. A lot." She stroked my head.

"I know. I can see it. And I still want to meet her."

I didn't want to share just how much I liked Stella. Not yet.

"I'll ask her about it." I was going to put that off as long as possible.

Mom looked down at her wedding ring. "I fell in love with your father when I was fourteen, so I know that it can happen when you're young and that it can last. Even if I could have dated around and gotten married later, I wouldn't have picked anyone else." I wouldn't pick anyone else but Stella, but it was impossible to know the future.

"Anyway, I just wanted to have that little talk with you. I love you, honey." I leaned in and she gave me a hug.

"I love you, too." She didn't mention anything about pot smoke and I scurried away to change my clothes.

***

"So, is this our first real date?" I asked when Stella picked me up the next day. I'd told my mom where we were going and when we were going to be back and she hounded me again about having Stella over for dinner so I guess that was going to happen sooner rather than later. My mom was persistent.

"I don't know. Do you count last night?" Shit. Last night. After I'd gone back to my room I'd undressed and thought about kissing Stella as I got myself off.

Four times.

"I don't know. Let's see how today goes and then we'll decide." I turned on the radio and flipped through the stations.

"But we need to know the anniversary of our first date so we can celebrate." Good point.

"Okay, last night can be our first date and this can be our first date-date." I found the pop station and hummed along to the current song that was playing twenty-four seven.

"What's a date-date?" We argued about that for the rest of the way to the movie theater. I bought the tickets and Stella got the popcorn and sodas.

"I can't believe we're doing this," I said, taking the popcorn from her and handing her a ticket.

"We're dating just like normal people."

"I know, right?" We laughed and headed into the theater.

The movie was one of the latest romantic blockbusters. I hadn't really cared about seeing it, but I figured if we weren't watching the movie, we could potentially make out in the back of the theater.

"Let's sit back there," I said, pointing to the last row of seats. There were only a few people and they sat way up front, so we were pretty alone back there.

"I know why you want us to sit back here and I completely approve of it," Stella said, sitting down and putting her soda in the cup holder.

"Good. I was hoping you would." I popped a piece of popcorn into my mouth and smiled at her.

"Don't eat it all," she said, shoving her hand into the tub.

"I'll share because I love you." I tilted the tub toward her and she smiled.

"Aw, you're so sweet. You're trying to out-sweet me." We had nearly finished the popcorn by the time the previews started. Stella pulled some wipes out of her purse and we cleaned the fake butter off our fingers.

She leaned over and I put my arm around her.

"I've never done this before. Not even with a boy," she said, leaning closer.

"Me neither," I said watching her eyes glow from the light of the screen.

She kissed me softly and then turned to watch the movie.

I just wanted to watch her, so I did. Half of my attention was on the movie (which was very heterosexual) and half was on her. The way she smiled, the way she laughed, how she concentrated.

"Stop staring at me," she whispered at one point.

"Can't help it," I said. She smirked and then reached her hand over, sliding it slowly up my thigh. I went rigid in my seat and Stella laughed softly next to me.

Shit.

Her fingers leisurely walked their way up my leg and stopped on the top of my thigh. She squeezed gently and then withdrew her hand.

"You are evil," I whispered. "I'm going to get you for that."

"God, I hope so."

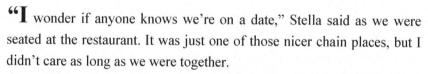

"I wonder if anyone knows we're on a date," Stella said as we were seated at the restaurant. It was just one of those nicer chain places, but I didn't care as long as we were together.

"Probably not. They just think we're friends." I looked around, but no one was paying attention to us.

"I could kiss you and then that would make things clear. Or we could sit on the same side and feed each other." I made a face.

"I love you, but I draw the line at feeding each other. Unless it's like, chocolate strawberries or something." Her eyes lit up.

"Ohhhh, that would be sexy. We should do that for our anniversary or something." I thought the anniversary talk was a little premature, but it was really sweet that she thought that way.

Our server came over and took our drink orders and asked if we were ready to order food.

"I think we'll have the spinach and artichoke dip as an ap, right, baby?" Stella said, winking at me. The server, a guy who probably wasn't much older than us looked from Stella to me and his face went red.

"Sure, babe. That sounds good," I said, grinning at her. The guy stuttered that he was going to put that order in. We waited until he left before we started laughing.

"I think you just gave that guy a heart attack. You're so bad." Stella shrugged.

"If he's scared by lesbians than I have some bad news for him. We're everywhere." I snorted.

"So, what did you think about Tris and Polly? They're really cute, right? I think we could be friends with them," I said and Stella put down her menu.

"Polly is adorable. I feel bad about Tris, though. I can understand why she was a little suspicious of us at first." It was a reminder that not everyone was as accepting as our friends and families.

"I think we could be friends with them. It would be nice to have gay friends." I agreed.

I told her about my mom's little "talk" she'd had with me last night and she laughed.

"My dad hasn't said anything to me. I guess he figures that since I'm going to be in college he might as well not bother." I wish my mom had felt that way.

"Has she backed off about the practice essays?" she asked me after we ordered our food.

"Not at all. Her new idea is to have me write about being gay. She thinks they'll be more eager to accept me because of 'diversity.'" I put the word "diversity" in air quotes.

"She did not."

"Swear to God. And I might actually do it. I mean, I have a lot of things to say about and it's better than writing something stupid that I don't care about." Our dip came and Stella dove for the first chip.

"That's a good point. Maybe I'll take a leaf out of your book." I snorted.

"I'll let you take a leaf out of my book anytime, baby." Stella threw a chip at me.

"That was a terrible innuendo."

"Made you think about me naked, though, didn't it?" Her face went red.

"Everything makes me think about you naked, Ky."

CHAPTER 18

Stella

I finally agreed to go over to Kyle's house for a dinner with her family on Sunday. I figured the sooner I got it over with, the better.

Kyle opened the door and gave me a nervous smile.

"Don't freak out," she whispered as she held the door open.

"Stella, it's so nice to officially meet you," Kyle's mom said. "You can call me Kate and this is my husband Cody." I shook both of their hands and gave Kate the flowers I'd picked up at the grocery store on the way over. I figured it couldn't hurt to suck up a little.

"These are lovely, thank you," Kate said as I followed Kyle into the living room. After Kate put the flowers in some water, we all sat in the living room and I prepared to be grilled.

Kyle took my hand and squeezed it. I stole a glance at her parents, but they didn't seem too upset.

"So, Stella, Kyle says you're a big reader," Kate said.

"Yeah, my father's an English professor so it was kind of inevitable." I laughed a little nervously and then Kate started asking me about my favorite books and that opened up a book discussion and I finally started to relax.

Dinner was roast chicken with mashed potatoes and salad and it went off without a hitch. Kyle kept squeezing my hand under the table to reassure me that I was doing okay.

"What are your college plans?" I'd been hoping I could get out of this dinner without talking about that, since it was a sore spot for me and Kyle.

"I'm not sure yet. My dad doesn't really care where I go as long as I study something I care about." Kate and Cody shared a look. I knew that wasn't their philosophy when it came to Kyle, but I wasn't going to lie.

There was a bit of an awkward silence until Kyle asked for her mom to pass the potatoes and then mentioned that I was a cheerleader, so they started asking me about that.

"Mom?" Kyle said as we cleared up the dishes and took them to the sink. "We're going to hang out in my room, okay?"

"Keep the door open!" she called from the living room.

I gave Kyle a look and she winked.

———————◆◆◆———————

"Are we ever gonna talk about college?" she said as we both sat on her bed, me at one end and her at the other. Just in case her mom decided to drop in with a plate of cookies or something.

I looked up at her ceiling.

"How about we not?"

"Baby, why don't you want to talk about it?" Wasn't it obvious?

"Because it makes me think about us being over." She stared at me.

"Why? Because we might go to different schools and then break up?" Obviously.

"It's just . . . it's not realistic." She rolled her eyes.

"That's bullshit and you know it. We're not other people. We're us. And we love each other."

"So?" I said.

"So?! That's the whole point!" Her mom walked by and poked her head in.

"Everything okay in here?"

"Yup, just fine," Kyle said, her voice on edge. I gave her a smile and she left heading back to the living room.

"You wouldn't even consider going to the same school?" she asked, picking at one of her pillows.

"That seems like a recipe for a breakup."

"Okay, so should we just break up now and save ourselves some time?" I groaned.

"That isn't what I meant." She hugged the pillow to her chest.

"Then what *do* you mean?"

"I mean that I don't want to talk or fight about this, which is why I've been avoiding it for so long."

Silence fell over us.

"I'd want to go where you go," she said quietly.

"Yeah?"

She looked up.

"Of course. I figure one college is pretty much like the next and I don't think wanting to go to the same place as the girl I love is a stupid reason to pick one school over another. People pick schools for a lot worse reasons." She did have a point there.

"But what if it doesn't work out?" She stared at me and I was uncomfortable with the intensity in her eyes.

"And what if it does?"

I didn't have an answer to that.

Things were a little weird after that conversation, so I decided to head home sooner than I might have. I had a lot on my mind, but I still gave Kyle a kiss goodbye and told her I would text her later in that night.

Dad was home and in the living room with a book, as usual. He looked up and must have seen the look on my face.

"What's wrong? Did the dinner not go well?" I sighed and crashed on the couch, leaning back and closing my eyes. It felt like this day had lasted forever. I was exhausted and it wasn't even eight.

"No, it did. Kyle and I had a little bit of a fight about college. She doesn't see a problem with picking a college based on where I'm going and I think that's a recipe for disaster." He put a bookmark in his book (no dog-earing pages. Blasphemy!) and set it down.

"Why do you think it's a recipe for disaster?" Was he serious?

"Because it's not a good reason to pick a school." He gazed at me.

"Why?"

"Because it's not!" Why couldn't anyone understand this? It was a known fact.

"It seems to me that making a decision based on what matters most to you would be the best way to go. So perhaps making a list of the things that matter to you might be a valuable exercise." I opened my mouth to argue, but then all I could think of was Kyle and I making the list of reasons that girls were better.

"But what if it ends?" I said.

"What if it does? You can always transfer, or, if you're at a big enough school, it might not even be an issue. I'm not telling you to go one way or the other, but what I don't want you to do is make a decision based on what you think you're *supposed* to do instead of what you *want* to do." I gaped at him.

"I don't want you to look back on your life and wish you'd been bolder with your decisions. Just think about it before you decide." Huh. I didn't know what to say. I just sat there for a few minutes and then told him I was going to take a shower.

I started making my list as the hot water poured down my back.

What did I care about? Kyle, obviously. A good English program. I didn't particularly care about the campus size, or if it was in a city or rural. I didn't care about activities, although if they had a cheer program, that would be an upside. I guess I just wasn't that picky. I'd already looked through brochures and online, but no place had really screamed at me. They all pretty much looked the same.

So if they were all the same, how was I going to make a decision?

I braced myself against the shower wall and thought until the hot water ran out. Shivering, I got out and wrapped myself up in a towel. Even though it was still early, I put on a pair of shorts and a tank top and got into bed. I texted Kyle that I loved her and goodnight and she sent me a kissy face.

I scrolled through the pictures of her that I had on my phone. They made me smile and laugh and wish I was with her.

Was I refusing to consider going to the same school just to be stubborn? Was I depriving myself of being happy for no reason?

I thought about it all night.

The morning didn't bring clarity, but it had distracted me from remembering that it was the Monday after the barn party and everyone was probably going to know that Kyle and I were together. I texted her to meet me by my car, as we'd planned.

"Hey, I was worried about you last night. Are you okay?" she asked when she got out of her car and hugged me.

"Yeah, just thinking about a lot of stuff. You ready for this?" She kissed my cheek and took my hand swinging it with hers.

"You bet, baby."

So we got a few yells, a few lewd comments, and a few gay slurs shot at us. Kyle just squeezed my hand and we kept walking together until we had to part to go to our separate homerooms.

Kyle kissed the back of my hand and said she'd see me at lunch and I went off to class.

I got more comments from people in class, but they were such poor attempts at insults that I just let them roll off my back.

Kyle texted me asking how it was going and I sent back that it was nothing I couldn't handle. Actually, those years of psychological torture had really prepared me for dealing with homophobia. Guess I should go back and thank the bullies for toughening me up.

All in all, most people didn't seem to care. Those that did had short attention spans and got distracted or ran out of insults when they saw I wasn't bothered by them.

Kyle and I met right outside the cafeteria with Midori and Grace. The two of them had struck up a friendship independent of us, which was great. No stress about them getting along.

Instead of me sitting with the cheerleaders and Kyle sitting with her friends, we found and empty table and claimed it. Grace and Midori joined us, followed by several of Kyle's friends (some of whom kept giving me wary looks) and surprisingly, Tris and Polly. A few of the cheer girls kept looking over as if they wanted to join, but they stayed where they were. I didn't mind. As long as I had Kyle and Midori, I had who I needed.

"You don't seem like a lesbian," Molly's boyfriend Tommy, said. She admonished him.

"What? She doesn't."

"And what does a lesbian 'seem' like?" Tris asked, narrowing her eyes.

He opened and closed his mouth a few times and then mumbled

something.

"That's what I thought," Tris said. "Anybody else have questions?" Everyone looked really uncomfortable.

"Okay, if no one will ask, I will. How does scissoring work?" Grace asked. I burst out laughing and so did everyone else. Even Tris cracked a smile. The tension was broken and the rest of the time was much less hostile.

"You're welcome," Grace said in my ear.

———◆———

"So that wasn't so bad, right?" Kyle said as I met her by our cars in the parking lot. Cheer practice had been cancelled so we were going to hang out together.

"Not really. I have to say, people aren't very creative with their lesbian insults. I got the same ones over and over. They really need better material." She snorted and put her arms around me. We rocked back and forth.

"Oh, I love you, my sexy cheerleader."

"I love you, my cute nerd."

We hadn't talked about the college thing today and I had the feeling Kyle was purposefully avoiding it. We were going to have to discuss it at some point, but not today.

"You wanna go makeout in my car?" she asked and I jerked back from the hug to find her wiggling her eyebrows.

"Hell, yeah."

Making out solved most problems.

———◆———

I was trying to give her some space on the college thing. I really thought that she was going to come around if I let her think it through. I didn't really want to tell her that I was going to end up at an in-state school, or a private school that gave me the best financial aid package. She didn't have as many restrictions. It would be totally different if she had a dream school she'd always wanted to go to and I would somehow keep her from that. She'd always talked about college in general terms and I knew she didn't have a preference. So why not go together?

We could even be roommates, which would just be awesome. Then we could make out in her bed or my bed, or even push them together. I was trying not to get ahead of myself, but I definitely couldn't stop thinking about it.

Now that we had tackled all the hurdles (so far) to be together, it seemed foolish to put more obstacles in our way that didn't need to be there.

But I was patient. I could wait for her to get there. And while I waited, we could just make out a lot.

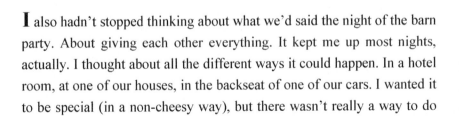

I also hadn't stopped thinking about what we'd said the night of the barn party. About giving each other everything. It kept me up most nights, actually. I thought about all the different ways it could happen. In a hotel room, at one of our houses, in the backseat of one of our cars. I wanted it to be special (in a non-cheesy way), but there wasn't really a way to do that. Unless I lied to my parents, which I really didn't want to do.

So I was out of ideas. I even looked shit up on Tumblr, but that was no help. If only one of us had an apartment.

There were a few times over the next two weeks where we got very, very close. We'd gotten shirts off, but hadn't gone further than that. Either one of us had put the brakes on, or we'd been interrupted for whatever reason.

"What do you think my parents would say if I told them I was sleeping over at Stella's?" I asked Grace when we were hanging out while Stella was at work.

"They would probably say no. But maybe not? If you're really mature about it, who knows?" That was true. She'd told me to be careful, but maybe . . .

The potential of being with Stella for the night was enough for me to get up the courage to ask.

"Mom?" She was in the midst of making dinner and Dad was still at work.

"Yes, honey?"

"What would you say if I asked to sleep over at Stella's?" She froze with a carrot and a peeler in her hand.

She inhaled through her nose and set both the carrot and the peeler down, bracing herself on the counter.

"I'd say . . . I don't know. I know you're both eighteen and technically adults, but I'm not sure I'm ready to condone . . . that . . . either." She finally looked at me.

"I figured. But I wanted to do the mature thing and ask. I would never go behind your back." She gave me a tight smile.

"I'll think about it. Okay? I promise to think about it." That was good enough for me. It wasn't a no.

"Thanks, Mom." I gave her a hug and asked if I could give her a hand.

A few days later Stella and I were laying side-by-side on her bed just staring at each other. I never knew how good that could be. Just to lay and breathe next to another person.

"I asked my mom if I could sleep over," I said as she walked her fingers up and down my arm.

"You did? Are you nuts?" I shrugged my shoulder.

"I didn't want to sneak around. Because then if we got caught, I wouldn't get to see you anymore. And that's not worth risking. I'd rather have some time than no time. That would kill me." She nodded.

"Agreed. What did she say?"

"The jury is still out. I haven't brought it up again, but I think she might say yes." Stella raised one eyebrow.

"Oh, really? And what if she said yes? Would that mean what I think it would mean?" I grinned.

"Yes, indeed." She threw her leg over mine and moved a little closer.

"So I should get some candles and some fancy sheets and maybe some lingerie?" I almost died at the thought of her in lacy lingerie.

"As long as you don't care about my non-sexy underwear." I had never owned anything made of lace. My undies were utilitarian, not sexy.

"Ky. It's not the underwear I want to see. It's what's *under* the underwear." I giggled.

"I guess you have a point."

"So, you think you're ready?" She pressed her forehead against mine.

"Yeah. Are you?" She bit her bottom lip and said one word against my lips.

"Yes."

Three days later, my parents sat me down and told me they would let me sleep over at Stella's.

"As long as you are careful, and you are responsible, and are where you are supposed to be when I call or text. I don't want to find that you two have run off to Vegas or something." I laughed at that, but she was serious.

One of the reasons I even existed was that my mom's parents had forbid her from seeing my dad, so they'd gone around their backs and "been irresponsible." I mean, she didn't put it that way, but it was the implication. Fortunately, Stella couldn't get me pregnant, so that wasn't one of their worries. And since neither of us had been with anyone sexually, we were pretty safe in that department too.

"Sex brings out a lot of emotions. I just want you to be ready for that, but if you tell me that you are, then I believe you," she said. Dad had let her do most of the talking, but had added his two cents here and there. I really wanted to stop talking about sex with my parents, but I sat and listened until they had talked themselves out. Then I scurried to my room to text Stella that all systems were go.

She'd also asked her dad if it was okay, and he had reluctantly agreed. It was a little weird knowing that both sets of our parents knew we were having sex. Or that we were going to. But that was the price we had to pay to be together. And in less than a year, we could do whatever we wanted.

Stella and I were still skirting the college issue, which was becoming more and more of an issue as colleges started sending reps to come and talk to us and convince us to attend their institution above the others.

I honestly didn't care all that much. College was college, I figured and I wasn't heading to an Ivy League, so what did it matter? Just seemed like kids went to fancy colleges so their parents could get a bumper sticker and brag in the Christmas letter.

I was going to wait until she brought it up, or there was a good time for it and I hadn't found that yet. I didn't want us to fight about it. We got along so well and I didn't want to provoke an argument if I didn't have to.

My dad is going away to a conference for the weekend she texted me the day after I'd given her the news about staying over.

You're kidding. That's like, perfect timing.

I know. It's like we planned it.

I couldn't stop the riot of butterflies that started beating their way through my stomach.

Guess I need to do some shopping . . . she texted back. I was going to die. I was going to die before she even got naked. Sex was going to kill me.

CHAPTER 19

Stella

My dad definitely knew what was going to happen when he was away, but he just gave me a look and told me to be careful. I told him I would and then waited for him to leave so I could get everything ready. I hoped she would like it. I'd made dinner (buffalo chicken lasagna, avocado and tomato salad, and a double fudge cake for dessert), cleaned my room within an inch of its life, made my bed with new 100 percent cotton sheets, and gotten cute lingerie that I was wearing under my adorable pink dress.

There were also candles and I had a playlist and everything. I'd probably gone overboard, but I didn't give a shit. I wanted this to be perfect.

An hour after my dad left, Kyle knocked on the door.

"Hey," I said, my voice squeaking a little as I looked at her. "Oh, wow."

She'd also put on a dress. A skintight black thing with a hint of gold shimmer. She'd also curled her hair and had mascara and red lipstick on. She was the sexiest bombshell I'd ever seen.

"Holy shit, Ky. Did you do all this for me?" She looked down at her feet. Still in black Chucks. It was so *her*, though.

"Yeah, and I'm freezing my ass off." She didn't have a coat on so I yanked her inside and she set down her backpack that presumably had a change of clothes anything else she might need.

"Well, you look hot as fuck freezing your ass off," I said, taking her hand and twirling her around so I could see the back.

"I wish you could see how your ass looks right now," I said and she turned back around.

"My turn," she said, shoving my shoulder so I'd turn around. I did a little twirl for her, my skirt flaring out.

"You like?"

She stepped close to me.

"I want to eat you alive. And I mean that in every way." I grabbed her face and we started kissing.

"I made you dinner," I said as she started to back me up toward my room.

"Sex first," she said.

"Okay, sure." I completely caved and then I realized that the oven was still on so I reluctantly pulled away so I could go and turn it off.

She stood in the hallway, leaning against the wall and waiting for me.

I stepped toward her, slowly, watching her watch me.

"Give me like five minutes," I said, brushing by her. She groaned, but nodded.

I rushed around my room and lit the candles and got the music going. Lot of Halsey on there. The first was a cover of "I Walk the Line" by Johnny Cash. It was slow and sexy and it made me think of her.

There was a knock at the door and I turned around to find Kyle in the doorway, a smile on her face.

"You didn't have to do all this," she said, waving her hand around the room. I walked toward her until we were only inches apart.

"I know. But I wanted to." I leaned forward and our lips met. She tried to move things faster, but I slowed her down. There was no rush. We had all night.

One step at a time, we walked together toward my bed and sat down. I ran my fingers through her curls, loving how they felt.

"I love you so much," she said in between kisses.

"I love you too," I said and turned so she could unzip the back of my dress. I pulled my hair out of the way and listened to the way her breath hitched as she realized what I wanted her to do.

Her fingers trembled as she gripped the zipper and drew it down slowly. I waited for her to push the straps of the dress off my shoulders, but then I felt her lips on the back of my neck, right where my spine started. She kissed her way down my back, following the line of my zipper. When she was done, she pushed off one strap, kissing the skin she exposed before doing the same to the other shoulder.

I pulled my arms free and stood up, pushing the dress down until it hit the floor.

"You're so beautiful, baby," Kyle said, sounding like she was going to cry.

As for lingerie, when I'd gone shopping I hadn't liked any of the fancy, elaborate contraptions that looked impossible to get in or out of. Instead I'd chosen a dark green silk bra and matching panties with a little lace on the edges. Simple.

Kyle stood and came to kiss me, but I stopped her.

"Now it's my turn."

I waited as she slowly peeled the dress off me. It got stuck a few times and we laughed.

"It's really tight," I said as an apology.

"I'll cut it off if I have to," she said, finally wrestling the dress over my head. "There."

I'd worn a simple black cotton bra and panties. I knew I didn't have to fancy myself up for her. She looked at me as if I was the sexiest thing she'd ever seen.

"Mmmmm," she said, running her hands up and down my sides, making goosebumps pop up. We backed toward the bed again and lay down next to each other just kissing. I was so afraid that if I slowed down, my anxiety was going to get the best of me.

I had no idea what I was doing. Sure, I could get myself off, but I had no idea what she liked. What she needed. What if I couldn't do it right? What if I scratched her? I'd cut my nails as short as I could get them.

"Ky. Stop thinking." Stella was staring at me. "If you don't want to do this, then we don't have to. Anytime you want to stop, you tell me. Okay?" She pushed my hair away from my face.

"Aren't you scared?" I asked.

"A little. The upside is that neither of us knows what we're doing. And I think I'm going to enjoy finding out what you like." She smiled and I realized I hadn't thought of it *that* way.

"Oh," I said.

"Exactly."

Our mouths met again and I let my hands wander across her body. So much skin to touch. So many places to explore and taste and linger over.

I got her under me and did exactly that until she was quivering under me and saying my name in a way that almost made me come.

She got me back with the same treatment and then we couldn't take it anymore and the lovely lingerie quickly ended up tossed on the floor.

I had no words for how beautiful her body was. None. I just lay there and stared at her. She was perfect.

Me, not so much. I tried to hide my leg, but she caught me.

"You're beautiful, baby. You're perfect." She scooted down and kissed my scars. Loved on every single one. It made me want to cry and then she slithered back up my body and stopped right at nipple level. Locking eyes with me, she very deliberately licked my nipple.

"Fuck, Stella." She laughed and then did it again. I was completely lost as she tortured one nipple and then the other until I was begging her.

"What do you want," she said, kissing down to my navel. "Tell me what you want, baby."

"You. I want you," I said, running my fingers through her hair.

"I know. Where do you want me?" She kissed down a tiny bit further and I was shaking.

"I'm scared." She stopped and rested her chin in my lower stomach.

"What are you scared of? Asking for what you want?" I nodded.

"Well, you'll never get it if you don't ask." She was torturing me.

"Why are you making me do this?" I whined and she laughed at my expense.

"Because I want to hear you say it."

I looked down at her, wondering if she was going to back down. She just lay there like she could wait forever.

"I want you to . . ." Ugh, why couldn't I say it?

"You want me to . . ." she said, waving her hand for me to go on.

I swallowed.

"I want you to go down on me."

She grinned.

"Oh, okay. All you had to do was ask."

I wanted to strangle her, but then she started kissing my lower belly, moving lower and lower until I almost told her to stop. She got close. So close and then stopped. I glared down at her, but she just smiled at me.

"Patience."

She scooted down and started from my knees up, kissing the

insides of my legs, traveling further and further toward where I needed her.

My legs quivered as she settled between them and gently pushed my legs further apart.

I almost jacked off the bed as she gently kissed me at the apex of my thighs. She put a hand on my stomach to keep me still and then the real torture began.

As if she had all the time in the world, she kissed me. Licked slowly, up and down, back and forth until I didn't know my name or what day it was or even what planet I was on. I had one hand in her hair and one gripping the blankets of the bed.

She might not have done this before, but she must have done some research because it was good. It was all good. Or at least I thought it was good until she sucked my clit into her mouth and then sneakily slid a finger inside me.

"Stella!" I gasped. "*Please.*" She continued to suck on my clit and move her finger in and out of me before adding another finger and then I couldn't take it.

I came so hard I saw stars and I thought my heart exploded. It went on for so long that when it was over, I didn't know if I was ever going to be able to move again.

"Where the *fuck* did you learn how to do that?" I said to the ceiling. I looked down to find her with a very satisfied grin on her face.

"Beginner's luck."

I was pretty proud of myself. First time going down on a girl and I made her come. I should get a star or something.

It took Kyle a little while to recover, but once she did, she attacked me and then I was the one begging and pleading.

"You don't have to," I said as she licked her way down my body.

"No way. I want to fuck you with my tongue and watch you come apart." I almost lost it just from that. She still had her glasses on and it was like all my fantasies were coming true in this moment.

Whereas I'd been gentler, she showed me no mercy, but it was exactly what I needed. I barely had to give her any direction as she sucked on my clit, hard, and thrust her fingers inside me, curling them to hit the right spot. It was wild and savage and I wouldn't have had it any other way. I came so fast that I didn't know it was happening until I was already in the middle of it.

"Oh my God, Ky." She kissed my stomach and crawled up to kiss my mouth. I could taste both of us and it turned me on so much that I was ready to go again.

We'd gotten the first rush over with, so we slowed down. Fucked each other at the same time. Tried different positions. Some were failures, but it didn't matter.

It was perfect and it was real.

Finally, exhaustion got the best of us and we both lay together, limbs entwined. She rested her head on my chest and I stroked her back.

"Should we try scissoring?" I said and she giggled.

"Why the hell not? I think we should try everything. I mean, not the weird stuff. You know, I saw a statistic that lesbians have the best sex lives. Better than heterosexual couples." I kissed the top of her head.

"Not surprised. Plus, we can do so many more positions."

Kyle's stomach chose that second to growl and we finally decided to have dinner. I grabbed a robe and tossed Kyle a long t-shirt I wore to bed sometimes.

"I just want to see you in my clothes," I said as she put it over her head.

"Ditto," she said and went to get her backpack. She pulled out a baggy t-shirt and athletic shorts and threw them at me. I put them on and took off the robe.

"Better?"

"Hell, yeah."

We'd worked up quite an appetite and we ate snuggled together on the couch, sharing one plate.

"You said we'd never feed each other," Kyle said.

"We're not feeding each other. We're sharing a plate. That's different," I said. "We each have our own fork. That's the difference." She didn't argue with me. We were both in post-orgasm haze.

"So, I made a decision," I said, stabbing a piece of cucumber.

"About what?" she asked.

"About college." She stared at me.

"And?"

I set my fork down.

"And I'm open to us going to the same school. Because you're the most important thing to me. More than having a cool campus, or anything like that. And there's nothing wrong with that." I'd thought about it until I'd sat with the decision for several days. I didn't get that bad feeling that I was making the wrong choice. All I felt was rightness, but I'd wanted to wait until tonight to tell her.

She took a deep breath.

"Really?"

"Really."

She set the plate down and tackled me.

"I hope your dad doesn't mind if I fuck you on the couch."

I shrugged one shoulder.

"What he doesn't know won't hurt him."

EPILOGUE

"**H**igh V! Low V! T! Candlesticks! Low V!"

I was struggling to keep up with Stella's instructions and finally messed up.

"I'm not good at this," I said, putting my arms down. For some reason, I'd thought it was a cute idea for Stella to teach me a little about cheerleading and we were starting at the bottom with motions, which were a lot harder than they seemed.

"Oh, come on, baby, you can do it." I pouted at her and she came over and took my bottom lip between her teeth.

"It's hard," I said when she broke the kiss.

"Well, how about we try something different? Lay on the grass." It was June and we were in her backyard. Stella and I were making the most of the time we had together since we both had full time jobs to help pay for college in the fall.

I lay down and then she told me to bring my knees up.

"Now what?" I asked and then she straddled me, leaning back against my knees.

"I enjoy the view?" she said, giving me a wink.

"You're terrible," I said, reaching up to tickle her. She squealed and rolled off me as I gained the advantage and tickled her until she breathlessly begged me to stop.

"Now who's on top?" I asked and she raised an eyebrow.

"You know what I mean," I said, grinding my hips a little.

"Mmmm," she said, holding onto my sides. "We can't fool around out here. The neighbors." I looked around.

"Eh, who cares?" I leaned down and shoved my tongue in her mouth.

The sunshine poured down on us and I was so glad that we didn't have to spend this summer saying goodbye. We'd both been accepted to the same school in Maine and were headed there in September. She'd chosen English as her major and I was still on the fence. We'd made lists, but I wanted to get to school and then figure out what I wanted. I had time.

We'd decided against rooming with one another, but our dorm rooms were only one building apart, so we'd be spending a lot of time together and maybe down the road we could get an apartment. Stella and I would figure it out. We'd already checked out the LGBTQIA organization so we could meet new people. In just a few months we'd become close with Tris and Polly and the other queer kids at school, but we were all headed in different directions next year. Still, Tris and Polly had given us an open invitation to visit them in Austin anytime and we were definitely going to do that on Spring Break.

I broke the kiss and looked down at my beautiful girl.

"I'm so glad your dad forced you to take AP English," I said.

"Let's *not* talk about my dad while we're making out." I snorted and watched how the light sparkled in her hair.

"Good plan." I pushed my glasses up my nose and she sighed happily.

"I love you, Ky."

"Love you too, baby."

ACKNOWLEDGMENTS

This is my first f/f book and I never thought I would be writing it. But here I am, writing the story of my heart and I wrote this book for me. I wrote this book for the girl who thought she was straight for 29 years. I wrote it for the girl who couldn't seem to find the right boy. The girl who was so deep in denial, she was drowning in it. The girls who, *at last*, figured out her own truth.

I wrote this for me and there was not a minute of writing this book that was work. I loved every single second of this (not that I don't love all writing, but some books come easier than others). This book was like breathing. And I'm so happy I got her. I'm so happy I made it to this point in my life. I'm so happy to be myself. Finally.

Thanks go to my editor, Laura, who worked her butt off and kept me laughing with her comments. My formatter who always works overtime (sorry!). My publicist who was completely on board and didn't bat an eyelash when I said I was writing f/f. My cover designer who put up with me asking her to make Stella's hair the perfect color. Queer Twitter for being my saving grace and my sanity and my support system. You all have NO idea how you've helped get me through some of the worst days. Thank you so much for loving my teasers and begging and pleading for this book. I couldn't have done it without you.

One last thing: If you are struggling with your sexuality/gender, I want to say one thing. YOU ARE NOT ALONE. You are NEVER alone. There are thousands of people online that are there and going through the same thing. Even if you are scared to reach out, follow people on Tumblr or Twitter or Facebook. Even if you are the only queer person in your entire town, you are not alone online.

If you are looking for other LGBTQIA books, LGBTQ Reads is a great resource.

Some of my favorite LGBTQIA books are:

Dating Sarah Cooper by Siera Maley
Out on Good Behavior by Dahlia Adler
The Scorpion Rules by Erin Bow
Cam Girl and Black Iris by Leah Raeder/Elliot Wake
The Gravity Between Us by Kristen Zimmer
Santa Oliva by Jacqueline Carey
Ash by Malinda Lo
Wildthorn by Jane Eagland
The Captive Prince by C. S. Pacat
Complimentary and Acute by Ella Lyons
A Fashionable Indulgence by K. J. Charles
Leveled by Jay Crownover
Everything Leads to You by Nina LaCour

*If you are an educator/librarian/work with LGBTQIA teens in the United States and would like a paperback copy of this book for your library/collection, please contact me (chel.c.cam@gmail.com) and I'd be happy to donate one to your school/organization.

ABOUT THE AUTHOR

Chelsea M. Cameron is a YA/NA and Adult *New York Times/USA Today* Best Selling author from Maine. Lover of things random and ridiculous, Jane Austen/Charlotte and Emily Bronte Fangirl, red velvet cake enthusiast, obsessive tea drinker, vegetarian, former cheerleader and world's worst video gamer.

When not writing, she enjoys watching infomercials, singing in the car and tweeting. She has a degree in journalism from the University of Maine, Orono that she promptly abandoned to write about the people in her own head. More often than not, these people turn out to be just as weird as she is.

Made in the USA
Coppell, TX
21 November 2020

41834214R00144